Karmyn
A Story of Hope

Lisa Washington

DEDICATION

To my Sorority Sisters, Iota Phi Lambda Sorority, Inc.
Nu Chapter, Savannah, GA

Am I my Sister's Keeper?

Be joyful in hope, patient in affliction, faithful in prayer.
Romans 12:12 NIV

ACKNOWLEDGMENTS

The Lord Almighty

My Husband, My Love

All My Sisters (in Love, and in Christ)

Ivy League Productions

Pastor Rickey and Robyn McCray

Taura White

Chapter 1

If it were possible, you would see steam rising from Karmyn. She was close to reaching her boiling point. Sitting in this conference room, at her attorney's office, listening to this man attempt to defame her character was driving her beyond angry. If he mentioned one more thing about money, she was liable to flip the conference room table over. As it stood, the negotiations were going nowhere, fast.

Karmyn's attorney, Alicia Waters, repeatedly tapped her pen on the table, creating an annoying clicking sound. That just increased the annoyance in Karmyn's head. Vincent and his attorney were whispering to one another. *Someone would need to speak soon, and it had better be Vincent's attorney*, Karmyn thought.

Karmyn and Vincent had married during their senior year of college. Karmyn worked as a tutor for work-study and had tutored many athletes. She had been Vincent's English tutor for three years and his girlfriend for two. Vincent was being talked about as the next best wide receiver in the game during his senior year of college, and he was ultimately drafted into the National Football League.

Now, they sat across from one another as enemies. Their marriage had lasted longer than most people thought. But those people didn't know anything about their relationship or history; and neither did Vincent's lawyer. Eight years they had been married, and two years they were separated.

"I think the suggestion that my client is offering is more than fair," Vincent's attorney finally spoke. Nicolas Butler, attorney to the stars, sat back in his chair and turned to his client. They both wore a smug smile that was making Karmyn want to vomit. Karmyn tried not to make eye contact with either man, but Nicolas had a way of commanding attention in the room. He sat there in his tailor-made suit, wearing monogrammed cufflinks and his Patek Philippe diamond watch, attempting to leave Karmyn in the poorhouse after this divorce.

Just thinking about the value of his watch was making Karmyn sick to her stomach. The watch was probably worth $25,000. He also drove a fancy sports car and enjoyed being seen out on the town with the hottest celebrity or fashion model. None of that gave him any reason to believe that Karmyn was only after Vincent's money.

Alicia responded to his absurd suggestion, "Well, my client is not satisfied…"

"She never is," Vincent said under his breath. Alicia tried to continue, but Karmyn had enough.

Karmyn stood and scrutinized Vincent from across the table. She was staring him straight in his eyes so he could see the anger and pain he had caused. "I won't accept anything less. I was worth it all." She grabbed her black leather Ashley Nicole designer handbag and stormed from the conference room. She needed to get away and get some air. She just needed to be away from everything that was happening in that room.

Vincent and his attorney were trying to negotiate an unacceptable deal. After the years she put into their marriage, the business she started, and then his infidelity, Karmyn deserved more than what he was offering. She rushed into the ladies' restroom and barely made it to the stall before she lost the contents of her stomach.

Alicia followed her to the restroom. "Karmyn? Are you okay in here?"

"Yeah, I'll be fine."

"Should I reschedule this meeting?"

"No. I want this over with right now. Can you get me a bottle of water? I will be right there."

Karmyn heard the door close behind Alicia and was grateful that she didn't ask any more questions. When this messy divorce was over, Karmyn would move on with her life and be just fine. Over the last month, she had lost weight due to the stress. The media was baiting at the bit for anything so they could report on the destruction of her life. She tried to throw herself into work, but that wasn't helping the way she hoped it would. Staring at a shell of herself in the mirror only confirmed that she needed to move on.

After a few more minutes in the restroom, Karmyn felt better. She held her head high and walked back toward the conference room. She stopped when she overheard Vincent's attorney say her name. He was in the hallway, talking to someone on his cell phone.

"Yeah, man. This woman thinks she is about to get the keys to the kingdom. All gold-diggers are alike. Nope, Gallagher says she doesn't know about the other women. Hopefully, she stops being overdramatic and comes back to the table. This is the best deal she is going to get. Let me get back in there before she comes back."

Karmyn held in her anger and tears as she watched Attorney Nicolas Butler return to the conference room. She did know about Vincent's women, all of them. She even knew about the baby Vincent wasn't claiming. All the more reason why she deserved everything she asked for and more. But Karmyn didn't want to ruin Vincent's life; she just wanted what was hers.

Her attorney convinced her that she deserved $15k in monthly alimony and half of his retirement pension when Vincent retired. All Karmyn wanted in this divorce was the 32,000 square foot house in Crescent View that she picked out and personally decorated. That house was supposed to be where she built her legacy and raised her family.

Karmyn also wanted to keep her business outright. Together, she and Vincent started Trium-Fit personal training gyms. But it was Karmyn who made it a success. She added the sports rehab and physical therapy aspect within the last two years. The years they had been separated.

Vincent hadn't as much as stepped one foot into one of the locations since they separated. She would not allow him to take everything she worked for. While he was with his women, she was building a business, a legacy.

Karmyn raised her chin, rolled her shoulders back, and returned to the conference room with a deep, cleansing breath.

"Finally, can we please get this over with?" Vincent announced upon seeing her return.

Karmyn took her seat next to her attorney and glared at both Nicolas and Vincent. She heard a voice in the back of her mind say, "*Vengeance is mine.*" The voice was clear as the cloudless sky she could see through the window.

Suddenly, Karmyn felt a chill course through her body, and an immediate calmness settled over her. Nicolas was about to speak when she interrupted him.

"You think you are so smart, don't you? The both of you are two peas in a pod. Arrogant and ignorant. Let this gold-digger tell you both something. I know all about your women, even the one who has your child. Knew about her when she was pregnant." Nicolas choked when she said, "gold-digger." Vincent had the nerve to look surprised. Karmyn continued, "I also know about the accounts in the Cayman Islands. Yes, both of them."

Karmyn stood, spread her hands across the table, and leaned over so both men could see the wrath she held inside. "I didn't ask you for anything but my house, my car, and my business. I don't want your money. Give it to Tawanna, or whatever your baby mama's name is."

She adjusted her purse on her shoulder, used her hands to smooth her skirt down and turned to exit the door. Before she left, she remembered to give Vincent something else to think about.

"Oh, and Vincent, don't forget about your mother's last will and testament. I didn't. I hope you never feel this kind of pain and betrayal."

Vincent's face dropped when she mentioned his mother's will. Velma Gallagher feared her son would be just like his rolling stone father with families all across the city. She left a provision in her will that said if Vincent were to have children outside of his marriage, he would have to forfeit his entire inheritance to the sum of $45 million to his first wife. She called it the First Wife Clause. Velma Gallagher was wiser than anyone ever gave her credit for. She kept her wealth a secret until the very end of her life. Most of her money was from an accident settlement years before Vincent was born. She invested the money and let it grow over 36 years to be paid out upon her death to her only son on his 40th birthday.

Karmyn inwardly smiled as she walked down the hall and out the doors of the attorney's office. She hoped Vincent would do the right thing. He needed to stop listening to his ignorant attorney. Vincent wasn't a selfish man, but Nicolas Butler got it into his head that he wouldn't have to pay her a dime due to the weak pre-nuptial agreement they had drafted before they married. Well, Mr. Butler didn't know about his mother's will. That was Karmyn's ace card.

*****

Nicolas looked to his client and asked, "What is she talking about?"

Vincent issued a series of expletives then dropped his head into his hands. "Give her whatever she wants." He grabbed the stack of documents sitting on the table in front of Alicia and signed every page where there was a colored sticky note. Then, he quietly stood and left the room the same way Karmyn had.

Completely clueless, Nicolas stared at the back of his client as he dropped his shoulders and left the room. He had no idea what had just happened, but it was apparent Vincent had not been honest. One minute they were laughing about not giving in to the ridiculous counter-offer from her attorney. The next minute, Vincent crumpled and signed all of the documents against his attorney's advice. There was more to him than Nicolas knew, and the football star was not going to let him in.

When Nicolas had clients that kept secrets, he usually didn't keep them around much longer. He couldn't do his job effectively if the client lied or kept secrets. Nicolas's clients were athletes, entertainers, and anyone else who could pay his extravagant retainer fees. His law practice was successful because there was honesty and trust between his staff and his clients.

A few hours after the Gallagher debacle, Nicolas found himself in his therapist chair. His therapist was his best friend, Simon Sharpe, owner of several barbershops throughout the city, most of which were located in low-income areas. Simon's flagship location was in the middle of the most depressed area of the city. Simon enjoyed mentoring the youth in the neighborhood and providing a different outlook on life than what the streets offered.

"Why are you in my chair on a Friday night?" Simon asked.

The barbershop was closed, but Simon liked to do a thorough cleaning of the shop before leaving for the weekend. Saturdays are when Simon usually made house calls to his high-end clients. He and Nicolas shared several high-profile clients and usually tossed each other business.

"Had a rough day. The client completely switched gears on me in the middle of negotiations. Made me feel like a fool. He was holding something back that changed the trajectory of the settlement." Nick aimlessly scrolled through messages on his cell phone.

"I know how you hate that." Simon grabbed a broom and started sweeping around his station. "What else is bothering you, Nick? You have had bad clients before, but you never sulked."

Sitting up straight in the barber's chair, Nick said, "I'm not sulking now." Nick thought about the now ex-Mrs. Vincent Gallagher. She was feisty and apparently had heard him call her a gold-digger. She didn't want any alimony or spousal support, even though she was entitled to it. All she wanted was her house and car and to keep her business free and clear from him. In reality, she hadn't asked for much at all. It was her attorney that added in the dollar figures."

She was definitely different from the other women he had experienced in these types of cases. Somehow, Nick believed Vincent Gallagher messed up with this one. Karmyn Hammond-Gallagher was a keeper. Her classic beauty was refreshing to see instead of the face lifts and nip tucks that were common in his world. Nick took a sip from his drink, then noticed Simon standing across the room, staring at him.

"What are you staring at?" Nick asked, agitated.

"You. The face you just made. Somebody really got to you. What's her name?"

"It doesn't matter. She is off-limits."

Chapter 2

2 years later

Karmyn hated the downtown area, especially when she had to go into the municipal building to correct paperwork for her gym. The parking was horrendous, there were always long lines, and it seemed like the clerk hated her job and took it out on the people who needed help.

She had finally straightened out her issues with the revenue department and was ready to get back to her gym. Her house and her gym were the only places where Karmyn felt a sense of happiness. She had a training client in an hour who hated to work with any of the other trainers.

Karmyn began texting her accountant, letting them know the problem was fixed. Having been officially divorced for two years, she would have thought Vincent's name would no longer appear on her business documents. But, once again, she had to drag her divorce certificate out and prove that he did not have any stake in her business.

Just as she was hitting send on her text message, she ran into a solid figure, tripped and started falling backward. Fortunately, she didn't feel the floor. Instead, she felt an arm wrap around her waist and pull her close.

"Watch out, lady!"

Karmyn knew the voice well. It seeped into her mind at random moments, usually at night in her dreams. She looked up and was face-to-face with someone she had hoped never to see again. When he realized who she was, he immediately released her. Together, they both gritted through clenched teeth, "YOU!"

"Try putting your phone down and watching where you are walking," Nick said to her.

"If you were paying such close attention to your surroundings, you would have seen me approach," Karmyn countered.

"Nah, you can't make this out to be my fault. I was standing here waiting for the elevator. You ran into me. I hope you drive better than you walk."

"Arrogant, egotistical, annoying, sorry excuse for a man."

"Judging much?"

"Like you judged me?" Karmyn rolled her eyes in dramatic fashion showing her disdain for Nick. "Just stay away from me."

"My pleasure."

They silently waited for the elevator doors to open. Not caring if the elevator was going up or down, they both entered. Additional people entered, filling the space between them.

It was too late to exit when Karmyn realized she was going up and not down. She audibly sighed, indicating her frustration. Of all days, she would have to run into him. As the saying goes, when it rains, it pours.

The doors opened on the eighth floor, and most of the people on the elevator got off. Leaving an elderly couple, herself, and Nick. She glanced at him, and when their eyes connected, she quickly averted. Even after two years, she still had a bad taste for the entertainment attorney. But somehow, she couldn't get past his good looks and well-defined body.

He was an attractive man, tall like she preferred. Karmyn was 5'8 and almost six feet in heels. Being a personal trainer, she also noticed he was very well built, especially his broad chest and muscular arms that seemed to hold her up when she almost fell.

The doors opened again, and the couple got off on the tenth floor. When Nick didn't get off, Karmyn couldn't help but ask, "Isn't this your floor?" She needed to get away from him as quickly as possible. He smelled good, and the fragrance was playing havoc on her senses.

She also didn't like confined spaces. Usually, she would take the stairs in buildings. It was healthier and just overall better. But in this building, the stairs were for emergencies only, so she had no choice but to take the elevator.

"As if it's any of your business, I'm leaving for the day," he replied, never taking his eyes from his cell phone.

"Don't work too hard, do you?" Karmyn retorted.

"Why are you talking to me?" Nick asked.

The elevator car descended and began to rattle about halfway down. Ten seconds later, the car stopped between the fifth and sixth floors. Karmyn gasped softly, not wanting to show her fear in front of Nick.

"Don't worry, this is an old building. This happens sometimes. It will start moving again in a second." The second never came. After only one minute, Karmyn started staring at the panel, trying to find the emergency button.

"I have to get out of here. Where is the emergency button?" Karmyn frantically asked.

"Old elevator. It doesn't have one."

Karmyn was still holding her phone in her hand. She tried to make a call but wasn't getting a signal. Suddenly, she felt the walls closing in on her. She internally told herself to keep calm. Nick was standing in the corner reading something on his phone, seemingly unbothered by their situation.

"Can you call for help?" Karmyn asked Nick.

"Karmyn, it's been like 90 seconds. Give it a minute."

Just as he finished his sentence, the elevator started moving, but then it plunged swiftly for what felt like an eternity and jerked to a halting stop, tossing Karmyn across the car into Nick's arms. This time he didn't release her but held her close. She couldn't look at him because she would lose the cool she was still trying to keep.

*****

Nick had to admit, the second time the elevator stopped, he was a little more concerned. The building was old, and he had been stuck a few times before, but nothing like this. When Karmyn fell into his arms, it was just like the dreams that chased him for the past 2 years. She had a slim waist, and her body was soft up against his. Her hair smelled like roses. And briefly, he was remembering his dreams of holding her.

She tried to push against his chest, but when he saw the tears bubbling in her eyes, he refused to let her go. Nicolas recognized fear, but there was something more in her eyes. He had an overwhelming need to take care of her.

Before Nick could say anything, there was a voice.

"Hello, anyone in the elevator?"

"Yes. How long before you get this fixed?" Nick yelled toward the voice.

"Is that you, Mr. Butler?"

"Yes."

"It's Jimmy from maintenance. Seems to be a serious problem. We have called the fire department, but the overrides aren't working. We also called the elevator company. How many people down there with you?"

"Just myself and one other person."

"Ok. We will get you out in a jiffy. Hang tight."

Nick looked into Karmyn's tear-stained face and felt his heart break. He wanted to allay her fears, but even he wasn't sure of the outcome. Instead, he decided to get comfortable. Still holding on to Karmyn, he eased them both to the floor.

"We may as well get comfortable," he offered when he noticed a change in her features.

"I don't want to get comfortable. I want to get out of here," Karmyn again tried to release herself from his embrace.

"I don't want to be here either, but unfortunately, that decision has been taken from us." Nick gave her his dazzling smile that usually made women weak in the knees.

Amazingly, she stopped fidgeting and fighting him. She sat there in his embrace for several minutes before speaking again.

"I don't like confined spaces," she whispered.

"That I can tell. What happened?" Nick gently asked, not wanting her to get upset with his questioning.

"Not that it is any of your business, but I was locked in a crawl space when I was younger. We were playing hide and seek. I thought I had found the perfect spot. Well, my parents told us not to play in the house, so when I couldn't get out of the space, I was afraid I would get in big trouble. So, I didn't say anything. My sisters feared the same fate, so they didn't say anything for almost 2 hours. Karleigh eventually had to tell the truth because my mother was about to call the police."

Nick enjoyed hearing her talk. When she wasn't angry and yelling, she had a melodious voice that caused his heart to beat a little faster. She was wearing her hair in a ponytail at the nape of her neck. Her face was free from any make-up, making her appear much younger than he knew her to be.

"Can you let me go?" Karmyn asked, breaking Nick from his thoughts.

"Do you promise not to fall apart?"

"I promise," Karmyn gave him a weak smile.

He released her, and she moved to sit beside him. That shocked

Nick. He assumed she would have moved to the other side of the elevator. They sat in silence, each in their own thoughts. Nick was sure if she knew what he was thinking, she would pop him over the head.

The time seemed to pass slowly. The only sound to be heard was their combined breathing. Since they were stuck together, Nick wanted to tell her something he should have done years ago.

"I want to apologize to you. I made assumptions about you and what I said was completely out of line." Nick looked at Karmyn for any sign of emotion or recognition she had heard his words.

Karmyn released a slow breath. "Well, you know what they say about assuming. You know what bothered me the most is you didn't know anything about me. It was apparent Vincent wasn't truthful with you about anything regarding me or our relationship."

That was true. Once Nick had all of the facts regarding the Gallaghers, it was too late. Vincent had only given him half of the story and still kept many secrets that Nick's private investigator found out about much later.

"You're right. That's why I dropped him as a client right afterward. I don't like doing business with untrustworthy people. It makes me look bad," he responded with all sincerity.

"Whatever."

She used that moment to move further away from him. Nick immediately missed the warmth of her body when she was next to him. Even though he felt better getting that off his chest, he still felt bad because she still thought of him as an arrogant attorney who represented her ex-husband. He wanted desperately to change her opinion of him.

They sat quietly for a few moments, each in their own thoughts, with only their breathing to be heard in the confined space. Nick reflected on the past two years. He researched Karmyn for his personal satisfaction. She was a successful entrepreneur, owning the premier athletic facility in the city. Her target market was clients like his, primarily athletes.

Karmyn had a reputation for fast and efficient recovery for

injured athletes. Her business was thriving and had tripled since her divorce from Vincent. Nick admired how she was able to have continued success despite rumors that surrounded her and her marriage.

Nick started laughing at their predicament. How crazy was it to be trapped in an elevator with the person who hates you most? Over the years, she made it known how she felt about him. Though they rarely ran in the same social circles, they did have clients in common. Nick was glad she wasn't trying to beat him up.

"What are you laughing at?" Karmyn asked.

"This situation. You, me, stuck together." Nick glanced her way and noticed she wasn't laughing.

"Yeah, well, there is a lesson in this somewhere. I will have a long chat with God after this is over."

"Oh, so you're one of those religious types?" Nick asked and immediately regretted the question with the look she gave to him.

"Yes, I am a woman of God; a Christian woman. What about you?" she asked.

"I believe in a higher power. I'm just more spiritual."

This time Karmyn laughed. He didn't find his response funny at all. He grew up in church, and his family considered themselves Christians. He just felt he had time to devote himself to church and all.

"What's so funny?" he asked.

"When people say that, it usually means they were raised to believe in God but don't want to go to church or read their bible. It's a cop-out, you know."

Nick was taken aback by how well she read him. She must have met others who shared his belief. But somehow, when she voiced it out loud, it didn't sound as good. It was true; he didn't go to church anymore. His career was very demanding. And he didn't consistently read his bible, but he remembered some essential verses.

His feelings were hurt, and he responded, "You can believe what you want. I know who I am."

"But do you know whose you are?" She asked without looking at him.

They remained silent, each in their own thoughts. Nick was trying to figure out why he was hurt by what she thought of his religious spirituality. It wasn't like he said he was an atheist. He believed, just not in the traditional way.

After being stuck in the elevator for over thirty minutes, Nick noticed Karmyn failing at keeping control of her breathing. Her breaths were heavier and coming faster than they had before. He suspected that she was having another panic attack.

He stood to his feet and stretched. He had to do something to get her to calm down.

"Do you dance?" Nick asked, staring down into her face.

"What?" Karmyn said through labored breaths.

"I asked do you dance?" Nick hoped that this would help her think of something other than being stuck in an elevator.

"Why?"

Nick used his phone to play a song from his playlist. "I like to Chicago step and Detroit Ballroom. Do you know either of those?"

"No."

"Stand up, let me teach you." He reached out his hand to her.

She stared at his hand for several seconds before responding. "I don't think that is wise. Dancing may shake the elevator or something. I think we need to remain still."

His first plan didn't work. He returned to the floor and sat closer to her than before. She didn't move away, so he took that as a small win.

"Well, tell me about yourself. Since you said I don't know you," Nick asked. He wanted to keep her talking. If she talked, she didn't have time to think about how long they had been in the elevator.

"Not much to tell. I own a few fitness gyms. Was married, now divorced and almost lost it all thanks to you," Karmyn told him with added attitude.

She had a way of making him feel worse. He tried to apologize for the dig at her character, but she wasn't having it. Nick noticed her bravado was weakening when her hands begin to tremble. She quickly turned her head so that Nick wouldn't see her tears.

"Come here," he reached for her. "You are shaking like you've seen a ghost." She didn't move toward him, so he gently grabbed her arm and pulled her into his embrace.

"I need to get out of here," she whispered.

"They are working on it. We won't be here much longer. Tell me about the wedding plans. How is Karleigh doing? Simon is a nervous wreck." His best friend Simon Sharpe was engaged to her oldest sister, Karleigh. The two had met when Karleigh opened her hair salon next door to Simon's barber shop. A year later, they were combining businesses and getting married.

"The planning is driving me crazy. I take that back…Karleigh is driving me crazy," Karmyn giggled, thinking about her bridezilla sister. "She has to have every detail perfect, right down to matching napkins and tablecloths. Each floral centerpiece has to have exactly seven roses and seven lilies because those are her favorite flowers, and the two of them met on the 7th day of the 7th month. The whole thing is beyond maddening. I'm so glad I eloped."

Nick was shocked by that news. He had assumed since her ex-husband was an NFL star, they would have had a lavish affair. Knowing they eloped added a new layer to who he thought Karmyn was.

"I know what you are thinking. But no, neither Vincent nor I wanted a huge wedding. We didn't tell anyone for a few weeks after we married. At first, we wanted it to be a surprise, but I was actually afraid of my grandmother and what she would do when she found out. She can be very demanding with her traditions."

"Well, my mother has already planned my entire wedding for me. Not taking into consideration my bride-to-be may not want her help. She didn't get a wedding of her own, so she has to make up for it somewhere."

"Do you have siblings?" Karmyn asked.

"I do. Two brothers and neither of them are interested in getting married either. My brothers are 22 and 24. Both are graduates of Harvard Law School."

"Did you go to Harvard?"

"No. I went to Florida A&M," he beamed. "I am a proud rattler."

"So, you're not from around here?" Karmyn furrowed her brow when she asked.

"Nope. I grew up in Savannah, Georgia. After graduating from law school, I found my way to the big city to practice law. Thanks to Simon, I was able to get my first clients. Before that, I bartended at Swank and worked as a substitute teacher in the high schools."

"Humble beginnings. That's impressive."

He didn't know why that statement from her meant something to him. What she thought meant something, and Nick didn't have a chance to process those feelings. "Now you tell me, why own a gym? Were you a fat kid or something?"

Karmyn rolled her eyes at the stereotypical thought of gym owners. "I was an athlete. Played softball, basketball, volleyball and ran a little track. In college, I stuck to basketball and track. I was a nanosecond away from making the Olympic team in the 400-meter dash."

"Impressive." It was Nick's turn to be impressed. She was definitely in shape, but Nick would have never thought Karmyn was an athlete. Whenever he saw her away from her gyms, she was always dressed to impress. Stylish in every way.

"Yeah, I gave it all up for him," she lowered her voice. "And you know what the really sad part is? I overlooked all of the signs about Vincent early on. I just wanted to be his friend, not a girlfriend. He had enough women hanging onto his every word."

Nick felt her adjust her position in his arms but not pull away. Maybe he was finally breaking through her hatred for him. He felt good getting to know her and hoped she was seeing the real him in return.

Karmyn continued, "We didn't set out to get involved. That's why your gold-digger comment hurt so bad. I never wanted his money. The media and the trolls on social media have dragged me through the mud since I was 21 years old. But it never mattered because I was Mrs. Vincent Gallagher. Not those other tramps. I had his name and his ring. You know, he chased me for 2 years before I finally gave in to go on a date with him."

"Karmyn, you don't have to continue," Nick said in a soothing voice because he heard her voice start to crack.

"You wanted to know more about me, well here I am. I married Vincent Gallagher 2 weeks before the draft. We knew he was sought after, but neither one of us predicted he would go in the first round. Then, to get picked up by the home team. I was more excited not having to move across the country. The first time I caught him cheating on me was with a girl he graduated with from high school. Her smile was too big, and I thought her eyes were too close together. He swore nothing was going on. Then came his so-called cousin from St. Louis. She was downright petty and disrespectful. Vincent would never stand up for me around his women. I knew they thought I was stupid for putting up with it. But I kept telling myself I had the house, the cars, the stuff. I just didn't have the man.

So, I threw myself into something I was good at doing. When I opened my first fitness studio, I taught Zumba and other group classes. It then grew into a boxing gym. The guys that starting coming asked for specific equipment, so I found a way to make it happen. Later, players from the different professional teams began coming through. I don't know if that had to do with Vincent or not. That led to a membership type of gym that was opened 24/7 and catered to personal trainers. Right before I was done with Vincent, I had opened the upscale location in West Hendricks Hills."

Nick's heart was hurting for her. He could feel she had been holding this in for a while. Knowing how close the sisters were, he wondered why her sisters had not been there for her. He had seen the Hammond sisters in action when Karleigh's salon was vandalized. They were close and supported one another in everything they did. Nick pulled her in closer and held her as she continued talking.

"I came home to celebrate the opening of my new location and found a note from one of his women at the door. Very explicit. So, I poured myself a glass of wine, turned on some music and waited. He came walking in the door a few hours later, and I had the empty wine bottle in my hand. I looked him in the eye and said, 'you broke every single piece of me.'

He dared to tear up because he was guilty, and he knew I was done with him. We were together for over eight years. We made a home together. He threw it all away over some girl he met on the road. I built him up, made him believe in himself. His own family and friends didn't give a crap about him. I stood by him. He thinks he played me, but he played himself out of true loyalty."

Nick kept quiet. He honestly didn't have anything to say. His initial assessment of Karmyn was dead wrong. Now, he only wanted to see her smile. Each time their paths crossed in the past, she had a sadness about her that he felt he helped put there. Now, he knew she disliked him because he bought into the garbage that circulated about celebrity wives. None of it was true about Karmyn.

Chapter 3

They sat in silence for several more minutes before they felt the elevator do a little jolt, then suddenly begin descending. Nick released Karmyn from his embrace, and she stood to her feet and dusted her pants off, clearly relieved to end this entrapment. She had no idea why she told him so much about herself. She hated Nick for thinking the worst of her during her divorce proceedings and attempting to do the very thing other women had done while she was married–attacking her character and trying to diminish her self-esteem.

Karmyn watched Nick stand to his full height and stretch his limbs. She was aware of a mutual attraction that neither of them acted upon. His attempts to keep her mind from going into negative places were commendable. Karmyn was scared, and a few times, thought she may lapse into a panic attack, but he kept her talking. His embrace was warm and comforting; maybe that is why she shared so much with him.

The elevator doors finally opened to two paramedics standing by. After refusing assistance, Karmyn left the building without looking back at Nick. She faintly heard him thanking the maintenance guy and the other first responders as she quickly walked away. She needed to get a big breath of fresh air.

Being close to Nick was more than she wanted to handle. Karmyn found it difficult to remain angry with him when he was so attractive. He was slowly changing her mind about him. In the elevator, he showed he was caring. That was something she didn't expect of him. Thankful to be away from him because the cologne he was wearing had her on the verge of throwing herself at him.

Once in her car, Karmyn sat there collecting her thoughts. Nicolas Butler was still an arrogant attorney and had an ego larger than his client list. So, she couldn't understand her attraction to him. He was just like Vincent. That thought left a bad taste in her mouth.

*****

Nick hadn't made it to his car in the government building parking lot before his phone was ringing. He glanced at the phone and saw that it was the love of his life, his mother.

"Hey, baby," he answered the phone.

"Don't you 'baby' me. Save that for your one-night stands," his mother teased.

"Mom, come on now, you know you're my one and only baby girl." Nick loved his mother as much as he loved his sports car. But she was his first love, and that would never change.

"Your father may have something to say about that," she laughed.

"How are you and Father? Still married?" The question was an ongoing joke he had with his parents. Nick once heard his mother tell a friend that they wouldn't have anything else in common when her sons left the house. But that wasn't true. When Nigel moved out, their parents found a new lease on life and began traveling like crazy.

"He's not going anywhere. And, after 40 years of marriage, I ain't leaving either. We are stuck with each other. I'm hoping you find happiness and get stuck with someone soon. Representing all those high-profile divorce cases have you soured on the idea of marriage."

"Well, Mom, I've got to go." Nick tried to get her off the phone. This conversation was destined to take a turn for the worst. She would start naming women he should meet, and most of them lived in Savannah.

"Oh no, you don't." She knew his motive. "I called to ask if you are coming to the party and if you are bringing someone?"

His parents would be lavishly celebrating their wedding anniversary—nothing too small for the Butlers.

"Mom, of course, I will be there, but I don't know about a date," he answered her honestly. His mother would know if he were not honest. She had a sixth sense when it came to her children. They were never able to surprise her. Even his father would laugh at his son's attempt to sneak something past her.

"Listen, I'm only getting older. I need grandchildren."

Nick had heard this broken record before. He leaned his head back against the headrest and closed his eyes. She was relentless when it came to something she wanted. And right now, she wanted grandchildren more than anything.

"I'm sure Nathan or Nigel will assist you in your quest," Nick joked.

"You are the oldest, and you are the leader. You know they follow your lead," his mother continued.

That was true of his younger brothers. They looked up to him; and if he weren't married, they probably wouldn't be thinking about it either. As a matter of fact, Nick was sure his brothers had no desire to marry. Both were living the single life and loving every moment of it.

"Mom, I am not seeing anyone seriously right now. But when I do, you will be the first to know. Now, I really do need to get to work," he pleaded with her.

"You work too hard. I am glad you will be taking off a week to spend time with us."

"A week?" What in the world would they be doing for a week. Nick expected a weekend of festivities, ending in a fancy dinner…but a week?

"You didn't know. This is a week-long event. And you are expected to be in attendance. There are no negotiations in this matter. See you soon." She ended the call quickly.

Nick knew his mother set him up, and he couldn't tell her no. The men in her life spoiled her. Whatever Dorothy Butler wanted, she got. Except, maybe this time. He had no intention to bring a date for an entire week to his parent's anniversary party.

*****

Karmyn needed to talk to someone. She needed her sisters. It was the middle of the day, so she was sure Karleigh was at the salon. In less than 20 minutes, Karmyn was walking through the doors of Serenity Salon and Spa. Karleigh was the oldest of the four Hammond sisters. Karleigh, Kaleigh, whom they affectionately call "Poe," and Karmyn were all two years apart in age. Their baby sister Kyna was six years younger. They called Kyna "the oopsie kid" because of the large gap in their ages.

Karmyn's heart filled with pride for her sister, who had stepped out on faith and walked away from a business career to pursue her goals. Karleigh's passion was in beauty, hair, and fashion. She realized her dream after working for years in corporate America.

Being able to work in your passion was why Karmyn started her personal training and fitness business. Karleigh encouraged her to go after her dreams even before she opened her first salon.

Serenity was a bevy of activity. Karleigh now had six full-time stylists, and thanks to Simon and his upscale clientele, she also had her own exclusive clientele list. She was also working on her personal brand of beauty and hair products.

As soon as Karmyn opened the door, she was warmly greeted by stylists and customers.

"Hey, Sister. What brings you by today?" Karleigh hugged her and motioned for her to sit in her stylist's chair.

"I need some advice," Karmyn sunk into the seat and tried not to sound overwhelmed.

"You came to the right place. We are full of advice," Echo, one of the stylists said. A few of the customers laughed because Echo was known for giving terrible advice.

"Be careful, girl. The advice ain't always good," Echo's client added. That sent the entire salon into laughter.

Karmyn loved the camaraderie and sisterly love you always felt when you walked into Serenity. The feeling of home was something she tried to implement in her gyms. Unfortunately, men didn't want or need the same types of friendships.

"Can I play with your hair while we talk?" Karleigh asked, already using her fingertips to massage Karmyn's scalp.

"Go for it." Karmyn leaned back and allowed her sister to continue. This always relaxed her when they were younger. "I am attracted to someone I shouldn't be attracted to. He is arrogant and thinks too highly of himself. He reminds me so much of Vincent."

The salon got a little quiet. Most of the stylists in the salon knew she was divorced from Vincent. Their divorce had made major headlines at the time. Karmyn was a local celebrity for the wrong reasons. Ever since then, she had been trying to change her image. But people only saw what they wanted, and the media saw her as an angry ex-housewife.

"Do you have a type, girl? Like all the guys you date are the same?" one customer asked.

"No. I haven't dated anyone except for Vincent," Karmyn responded without opening her eyes.

The entire salon was quiet, hanging on to her every word. It seemed that the stylists even stopped working to hear her story.

"You have only dated one person, ever?" another customer asked.

"Is that so crazy to believe?" Karleigh jumped in to defend her sister.

The salon responded with a united "Yes," then they all erupted into laughter. Karmyn knew it seemed far-fetched, but she never dated before college, and Vincent was her first in every way.

"Well, I didn't date in high school, and in college, I was focused on my studies," Karmyn offered that as her reason.

Several of the ladies turned their heads away as if it were so hard to believe a woman would marry the only man she ever dated. Well, too bad for them, but Karmyn did exactly that.

"Sister, I understand. You don't want to fall into the same type of relationship with this new guy. But, you can't let that stop you from dating either," Karleigh offered. She then grabbed a brush and started brushing Karmyn's hair.

One of Whisper's customers asked, "Honey, is the man married? Is he unemployed? And does he live with his mama? If you say no to those three questions, then give that man a chance." A few ladies agreed with her.

Completely exasperated, Karmyn said, "It's just one minute he is so attractive, then the next I feel like I'm in a rerun of my old life. I can't go through the same things as before."

"Sister, you haven't even given this guy a chance. Is he even attracted to you?" Karleigh asked her.

"Karleigh, every man is attracted to you and your sisters. You ladies are gorgeous," Whisper said. Many of the customers agreed with her.

"Well, is he?" an older lady under the hairdryer asked Karmyn. "Do you know if he is attracted to you?"

Karmyn thought back to the hour they spent in the elevator and how Nick held her close and allowed her to spill her heart without saying anything. He just listened. "I don't know. I think he might be. He almost kissed me."

"What? When? Where?" the questions were coming from everywhere.

"Today, in the elevator at the government building. The elevator malfunctioned, and we were stuck together for almost an hour. I kinda had an anxiety attack, and he held me in his arms. And I liked it."

There was rumbling around the salon, but no one said anything loud enough for Karmyn to hear.

"Sister, there is nothing with liking being held in a man's arms."

"It is when the guy is your ex-husband's divorce attorney." Karmyn realized she may have said too much. It wouldn't be difficult for Karleigh to begin adding things up and figure out Nick was the attorney.

Before the salon could start asking questions, Karleigh grabbed Karmyn's hand and pulled her to the office for privacy. Karmyn realized it was time to come clean with her sister. She had never told anyone what happened in that conference room.

"After the divorce, I had seen him a couple of times here and there, but today I literally bumped into him." Karmyn told Karleigh about the dreams, the betraying thoughts and everything she shared with Nick in the elevator. She didn't tell her sister that the attorney was in fact Nick, her fiancé's best friend.

"Ok, you said it yourself. He is not all bad. Maybe you should stop being so angry with him. He was only doing his job," Karleigh said.

"Calling me a gold-digger is doing his job?" Karmyn asked.

"Forgive him his one mistake." Karleigh grabbed Karmyn's hands and looked at her. "This is going to eat you up inside."

Karmyn thought about what her sister said and how being mad at him took too much of her energy. Also, he had apologized, and he seemed sincere. Even telling her that he dropped Vincent as a client.

"I think you are right," Karmyn released her hands and gave her sister a big hug.

"Of course, I am. That's why you came over here."

"Well, if I ever see him again, I will talk with him. But what do I do about these dreams?"

"Oh, you will see him again," Karleigh snickered. Yep, Karleigh exactly who Karmyn had been fantasizing about.

The next day, Karmyn was working at her main gym facility. This was her first location and the largest in the city. Her administrative offices were in this building, along with the physical therapy offices. The building was secure from the outside, providing a sense of privacy for her A-list clients. You needed a key fob and a passcode to enter the gym. New clients met with membership associates on the first floor.

Karmyn sat in her office, attempting to review some financial statements. However, her thoughts were all over the place. First, she was worried about her sister. Poe grew up hating her name and chose something different, inspired by her favorite author, Edgar Allen Poe. Poe had been sick recently, and no one knew what was happening. Even the doctors were confused.

Then, Karmyn's thoughts shifted to Karleigh's wedding, then back to Nick. It seemed every wayward thought she was having ended with her thinking about him. Her dreams had not subsided. If it were possible, last night's dream was more vivid.

Nick was arrogant, but the few times she had seen him, he was also humble. How does he pull that off so effortlessly? Maybe her initial reaction to him was off-base. Maybe Vincent had told him lies about her that he believed she could be a gold-digger. It wasn't unheard of for a woman to attach herself to a potential athlete, get pregnant or marry him for a prosperous future.

Her thoughts were interrupted by a long crash, then an even louder scream. Karmyn raced from her office and found a gathering in the weights area. She pushed through the throng of onlookers to find Mr. Haney on the floor with one hand to the back of his neck and the other on his back. He was moaning and evidently in a lot of pain.

"What happened here?"

Amber, a trainer, was kneeling beside Mr. Haney. "He was working with the weights, and suddenly I heard a crash. When I turned around, he was on the floor."

"I'll sue you for this," Mr. Haney threatened.

Karmyn ignored his threat and asked Amber, "Were you working with him?"

"No, I was working with the group over there." She pointed to some ladies standing close by. They were observing from a distance. "I think he was working alone."

"This place is dangerous, and you will pay for this," Mr. Haney was still throwing out threats.

Karmyn kept her composure as she responded to his accusations. "Mr. Haney, I can assure you, your safety comes first."

Something was suspicious because Mr. Haney was near the light weights, and there were no obstructions that would have caused the man to injure himself. Nevertheless, her gym members signed contracts that included a clause about working with machines and weights unattended.

"The EMS has been called," another trainer rushed over.

"Mr. Haney, the medics are on their way. Please do not move. We want to prevent further injury," Karmyn cautioned him when he tried to stand.

"Further injury, so you can somehow skip out on paying for this." He pushed against Amber and tried to sit up, but the EMTs were walking through the door.

"Mr. Haney, please let the medics look at you," Karmyn pleaded with him.

The other clients began to dissipate away from the area as Mr. Haney was being attended to. This was all she needed, another problem that needed to be fixed. Once Mr. Haney was taken care of, she would need to retrieve her security footage to determine what happened. Karmyn used a security company that housed the videos at an off-sight location. Until then, she would need to wait and contact an attorney. She had no doubt, Mr. Haney would make good on his threat to sue her.

As the medics took Mr. Haney to the ambulance on a stretcher, he continued hurling threats at her. Karmyn tried not to pay him any attention. She walked with them to the front door and collided once again with a familiar scent and solid chest.

Nick was opening the door as she was coming through.

"You seem to have a problem not looking where you are going," he joked.

"Not now, Nick. I have to handle this situation," Karmyn exclaimed, clearly frustrated.

"What happened?" he asked, following behind her.

"I don't know just yet. Give me a minute," Karmyn told him.

Why was he here? In her space? It could be divine intervention. She had thought she needed an attorney. Her current lawyer was business and contracts. She doubted he worked on accident cases. Nick, on the other hand, handled just about anything.

Karmyn made sure that Mr. Haney was secure in the ambulance and headed to Metropolitan Hospital. She would check on him in a few hours. As she re-entered her building, Nick was patiently waiting for her. He was holding the door open for her and looking just as good as he had in her dreams.

"Why are you here?" Karmyn asked while continuing to her office.

"Because I wanted to see you," he responded, following behind her, trying to keep up with her pace.

"Well, as you can see, this is not a good time," she sat at her desk and opened her laptop.

"I think it is the perfect time. It looks to me like you may need my assistance."

Karmyn thought she would rather chew nails than ask for his help. But he was right. She did need legal advice at the very least. She gave him a curious look and stared, noticing how his suit was tailored to fit perfectly. His diamond cufflinks sparkled brightly as the sun streamed through the window. She probably wouldn't be able to afford him.

"I appreciate the offer, but I doubt I can afford your services." Karmyn turned to her laptop and began emailing the Security Guys to obtain the camera footage. When she hit send on her email, Nick was still standing there.

"What?" she asked, irritated to see him still standing there.

"I'm waiting for you to tell me what happened so that I can assist you. I never mentioned charging you a fee, did I?" Nick responded.

"Ugh! Fine. Sit down." Karmyn explained what she knew of the incident with Mr. Haney. And how she just ordered the video footage.

"Sounds to me as if you have an opportunist looking for a payday," Nick smoothly assessed the situation as told to him.

His statement hit a nerve with Karmyn. Even though she thought the same thing was happening, that was also the very thing he thought about her during her divorce. "I guess you would see it that way, wouldn't you? Everyone is out for something."

"I can't apologize enough for misjudging you, but in my experience, yes, everyone is out to get something. And, Mr. Haney seems the same way. How long has he been a member here?"

Karmyn checked his membership file on her computer and found out he had only been a member less than a month. He had yet to pay a monthly fee because he joined under a promotion. She looked up at Nick to see his smug smile looking back at her.

"Let's discuss this and what I came here for over coffee. There is a great place a few blocks over."

"I don't have the time." She looked into his eyes and almost agreed, but remember she was working and very busy.

"You have to take a break sometime. All work and no play makes Karmyn a cranky gym owner," Nick joked.

"Twenty minutes." And that was all she was going to give him. Anything longer may have her saying or doing something she would regret.

"Thirty minutes…let's go."

Chapter 4

Nick had silently been praying she wouldn't get angry about his assertive request for her to join him for coffee. He hadn't planned to see her at all today. The gym she owned occupied the first and second levels of an office building where he wanted to relocate his offices. It was pure coincidence that they ran into each again.

Without talking, they walked the two blocks to the coffee shop. The place wasn't crowded for a weekday afternoon, and they found an empty table near the back for privacy. He ordered two coffees and two croissants, then returned to the table where Karmyn read something on her phone that made her frown.

"Is everything okay?" Nick asked her. She looked concerned at what she was viewing.

"Yes. Mr. Haney is being evaluated, but it doesn't appear he has any serious injuries. I'm still waiting on the camera footage," she answered, sounding defeated. Nick hated to see her this way. Karmyn was one of the fiercest women he knew, and to see her this way was disheartening.

"Did Simon turn you on to the Security Guys for your surveillance?" Nick asked, hoping to lighten her mood. The Security Guys did work for all of Simon's barbershops and Serenity Salon.

"Yeah, they have been great," Karmyn answered with a genuine smile. "I wish I had known about them years ago."

That was the first smile he had seen from her. When they first met, she had no cause to smile during her divorce negotiations. Then, she was still angry with him afterward and later scared while being stuck in the elevator. Earlier, she had been concerned about a possibly injured client. Her smile was beautiful and caused a hitch of sorts in his chest. He suddenly wanted to see her smile at all times.

"Listen, I can take care of any lawsuit Mr. Haney may file against you if you do me a favor," he asked before taking a bite of his croissant.

Karmyn lifted her head from reading her cell phone and stared at Nick. "I knew it. You have an ulterior motive. What do you want?"

It shouldn't have shocked him that she would think the worst of him. But in this case, she was right. The idea came from out of left field. "I need a date to my parent's wedding anniversary party." He had no idea why he would ask her. For starters, she hated him.

"Absolutely not," she aggressively shook her head from side to side.

"Listen, you would be helping me out of a jam. My mother is trying to marry me off, and I want nothing to do with her suggestions."

"Why? Aren't they perky enough for you? Or do they have too much intelligence?" Karmyn slapped him with a case of his bad judgment in women. Before Nick could respond, she continued, "I don't think it will work. We don't get along."

"We seem to be doing fine now. And I thought we called a truce in the elevator." Neither of them said anything for a few moments. "We don't need to be in love or anything, just block for me. You know, to keep the other women away. And possibly get my mother off my back for a short time."

"Let me think about it." Karmyn began standing and reaching for her coffee. "Thanks for the coffee, but I need to check on Mr.

Haney and get back to work."

Nick stood with her. "I will check on Mr. Haney. As your attorney, I recommend you limit contact with him."

Karmyn arched an eyebrow at him, giving him the once over, making him feel like an art piece at auction. "Fine, but I haven't said yes or hired you yet," she responded.

"Duly noted," Nick gave her his signature smile.

He watched her leave the coffee shop and noticed how good she looked in her workout clothes. He supposed the uniform of the day for her would always include leggings. Somehow, he didn't like thinking about how she worked around all of those men wearing something so tight. The slight feeling of jealousy crept up, and Nick pushed it back down. The feeling was foreign to him, and he didn't like it.

Nick stayed in the coffee shop and thought about calling his mother. He contemplated telling her he was indeed bringing someone to the party. Telling her that would lead to questions he didn't have answers for. Dorothy Butler was a better investigator and interrogator than he or his brothers.

Later that afternoon, Nick couldn't stop thinking about Karmyn and why he suddenly was attracted to her. He had stopped by the hospital to check on Mr. Haney, only to find the man had checked himself out. The doctors didn't share much, but Nick gathered he had very minimal injuries, if any.

After leaving the hospital, Nick returned to the building where Karmyn's gym was located. He was seriously considering the move, especially if he could run into Karmyn on a more regular basis. The building was perfect. He would have the entire 16th floor, and a free gym membership came with the lease—just one of the perks of leasing in the building.

He signed the lease on the spot for purely selfish reasons. Even if the space had not been perfect, he might have signed on anyways. Just being that close to her was worth her possible fury.

At the end of the workday, Nick had other responsibilities. He volunteered at the youth group home on Monday and Tuesdays with Simon. Wednesdays he was on a local bowling team, Thursdays were usually set aside for his few evening meetings with non-profit organizations where he sat on the board. Friday was his day of relaxation. Saturdays and Sundays often included catching up on whatever he missed during the week or playing a few basketball games with the neighborhood guys.

This evening, Simon was expecting him at the group home because he led the men's talk with the male residents. Every month, the residents and several community members got together to discuss anything the residents wanted to talk about. Most months, the conversations ended with relationship talk. That was probably the last topic Nick needed to discuss.

*****

Karmyn needed her head examined if she was seriously considering attending an anniversary party with Nick. Especially a party for his parents. But, getting away for a while might do her some good. And it would allow her to see how 40 years of marriage worked. Give her some hope for the future.

She desired to be married again. The first time wasn't always bad. She did have some happy memories with Vincent. At one point, they were madly in love. He just loved the attention that came with fame more than he loved her.

Deciding not to think about her failed marriage or Nicolas Butler any longer, she dived into her work. Her second and third locations were doing well, above projections. Adding the physical therapy site seemed to be worth the investment. Karmyn had her head down and hadn't noticed her visitor.

"Hello, Sister!" Poe yelled from the doorway.

Jumping from her seat, Karmyn placed her hand over her rapidly beating heart. "Dang Poe, you didn't have to scare me like that. What's up?"

"I just thought I would stop by and see how you are doing. I know you have been working extra-long hours to stay away from Karleigh." Poe entered her office and plopped down on the sofa across from Karmyn's desk.

Poe had been right when she accused Karleigh of becoming a real bridezilla. Karleigh had been demanding of her sisters and annoying the wedding vendors. The majority of the planning had been completed, but that didn't stop Karleigh from wanting more. The last to-do items were the final fitting for Karleigh's gown and the bachelorette party. Kyna was the youngest and the partier amongst the sisters, so they tasked her with those details.

"Have you heard from Kyna on the party plans?" Karmyn asked.

"No, and that scares me. With an unlimited budget for this soiree, we may be jumping from planes or flying to Dubai."

The sisters recently found out that Kyna secretly married billionaire businessman Morgan Hawkins, who also happened to be the older brother Dr. Grant Hawkins, who happened to be pursuing Poe for a romantic relationship.

"Kyna has been very frugal with her newfound wealth. I think she will be conservative. However, little sister likes to party," Poe added.

"Right." They both laughed.

As if she had known they were talking about her, in walked Kyna.

"What y'all laughing at?" Kyna asked.

Karmyn and Poe looked at each other and started laughing harder.

"You have an innate talent for showing up when people are talking about you," Poe said after she stopped laughing.

"Talk about me if you want. I came by to discuss the plans for the bachelorette party." Kyna sat next to Poe on the sofa.

"No strippers," Karmyn begged.

"Please, sisters, Karleigh would kill me. I managed to get us a private yacht in Miami. We are staying on the yacht, and the other attendees will be at a boutique hotel on the strip. It's going to be fabulous."

The three sisters discussed the details of the party, and Karmyn was impressed by the restraint that Kyna was using. The yacht was being loaned to them from one of Morgan's business partners, and they were all being flown to Miami on Morgan's private jet. Other than those luxuries, Kyna was staying within a modest budget.

"I like everything you have planned. Great job, Sister," Poe applauded her.

"I agree. This looks like real fun," Karmyn agreed.

"Thank you very much. I bet y'all thought I was going to go crazy with spending, but I am being conservative. Morgan still thinks I am too frugal, especially after his last business deal was finalized."

"How are you two doing?" Poe asked.

Kyna and Morgan had married after only knowing each other one week. The marriage started a little rocky, and both acknowledged they hadn't thought through their decision.

"We are much better now. Counseling has been a tremendous help," Kyna answered.

Karmyn walked her sisters to their vehicles and watched them leave. She was incredibly proud of her sisters. Poe was a successful realtor whose business was launched into the stratosphere with her most recent clients. Kyna was also successful in working on women's infertility and reproduction research.

Even though each of them was madly in love with their significant others, Karmyn still hoped to find her happily ever after. Instantly an image of Nick came to mind. She tried to shake his image away, but his gorgeous smile was staring right back at her.

She must be crazy to believe there could ever be anything between them. Karmyn turned away from her building to head toward her vehicle and recognized the expensive sports car across the street at the valet stand to an exclusive restaurant. Frozen in place, Karmyn waited for the owner to show up. She didn't wait long for Nick to appear draped by a tall, lanky woman.

Chapter 5

It's showtime! That was how Karmyn felt when she had awakened that morning. Her oldest sister was getting married. The day was going to be perfect if the Hammond sisters had any control. But they all knew that only God was in control.

The wedding was to be held at their family church, and then the reception would be in the ballroom of the Greystone Manor Hotel. Karleigh made the entire wedding party stay overnight at the hotel. She didn't want anyone to show up late. Her main concern was with the men of the wedding party. Nick had promised not to throw a wild bachelor party for Simon, but the news was already spreading that security had been called three times to their suite. The men stayed in one of the luxury suites a few floors beneath the women in the spatial presidential penthouse suite.

Breakfast was served promptly at 9:30 am. The women were awake and partaking in complimentary mimosas. Kyna turned the music up loud to get the party started. Karleigh had six bridesmaids, her three sisters, and three other attendants who worked at Serenity. Echo and Whisper were fraternal twin sisters who were complete opposites in looks and personality. Jasmine was a stylist and esthetician; she was also the manager of Serenity West. Karleigh had recently opened Serenity East on the other side of town and had plans to open Serenity Downtown in the building with Karmyn's gym.

Each bridesmaid had her hair, nails, and make-up professionally styled. Jasmine had made sure everyone had a nighttime skin routine before going to bed the night before. While the hustle and bustle of the room was happening, Karmyn was only thinking of Nick. She had the bad luck of having to walk the aisle with him. She had hoped to be paired with one of Simon's fraternity brothers. She liked Dallas; he was married and not a threat to her sanity. All of Simon's groomsmen were extremely attractive.

Karmyn had been dodging Nick for the last week. She had got it into her mind that maybe she misjudged Nick. He seemed genuine in their previous few interactions. What she couldn't understand was why did he ask her to attend his parent's wedding anniversary? He had his pick of women who would probably jump at the chance to spend a weekend with him. She tried to live in the moment and not overthink about Nick and that woman.

Karmyn and Poe were the first to be finished with their beauty sessions.

"Karmyn, I'm going downstairs to check on things in the ballroom." Poe was the maid of honor and in charge of the reception. She had done an excellent job even with her health issues. Poe had been recently diagnosed with Lupus, and she had bad days that were painful for her.

"I can go down with you. Besides, I don't see how they can stand the smell in here," Karmyn motioned over to the other ladies. The fragrances of hair sprays, nail polishes, and perfumes were all blending in the worst way.

Poe laughed as she looked at the bridesmaid trying to instruct the hired stylists. "They are used to all of the hair spray fumes and nail polish. Another reason why I am getting out of here."

Dressed only in their short, personalized bridesmaid's robes, Karmyn and Poe headed for the ballroom. They ran into Grant, standing outside of the ballroom where the decorators were setting up. Not wanting to be a third wheel, Karmyn backed up toward the bar and ran into the man who was occupying her thoughts. He looked perfect dressed in an Armani tuxedo, clean-shaven and standing in front of her with that smile that would cause a woman to swoon. She quickly feigned annoyance at his interruption.

"Fancy meeting you here," he said.

Karmyn wasn't the least bit interested in his cheesy lines. She wanted to run away, but her feet remained planted in place.

"What are you doing down here? I'm sure Karleigh has some type of pampering scheduled for you guys," Karmyn asked, already knowing what was planned for the men.

"She tried it. We were on board for the facials and fresh haircuts, but all the guys drew the line at the pedicures. No clear paint on these toes," Nick laughed.

Nick took a step closer to Karmyn when she stepped back, and she momentarily lost her train of thought. Then like a wallop across her head, she smelled it. "Have you been drinking?"

"Not as much as Simon or Dallas," he laughed again.

"Karleigh is going to kill you. You are supposed to be responsible for Simon," Karmyn reprimanded him.

"He's not that bad, just a couple of beers. Nothing like the mimosas I'm sure you ladies have had." He was right. She had consumed about four drinks before leaving the room.

"Fine. She won't hear it from me."

Nick stepped closer, and Instead of moving back, away from him, she seemed to get closer. Out of nowhere, he leaned in for a kiss. Karmyn felt her headed spinning and thought her body was swaying back and forth. The kiss was potent, and the feel of Nick's arms around her waist felt right. She didn't want the kiss to end, and then she smelled her sister's perfume.

Karmyn snapped out of her daydream and stepped back, looking around the area. She didn't see Poe, but she was sure her sister had been there. Karmyn knew Poe had seen them kissing. That was the last thing she wanted her sister to know. Poe wasn't the sister to tell her business, but she would have questions. Like why was she kissing the man everyone thought she hated?

"I have to go back to the room." Karmyn tried to escape, but Nick was still holding her hand.

"Don't regret what just happened. It was good." He then released her and let her run away.

*****

Nick had to get his head examined. He was, again, lusting after the one woman he knew he shouldn't want. That kiss was everything, and now he didn't care if she should be off-limits. He was going after her, full force. He hoped she was ready for him.

The wedding ceremony was beautiful. The Hammond sisters outdid themselves, and they all looked so beautiful. The photographer had finished with the guys and was now taking photos of the women. Nick slid into the church pew behind Grant to view Karmyn. He heard Grant whisper, "She is gorgeous."

Nick smiled, knowing he was talking about Poe, but he was thinking about Karmyn.

"Yes, she is. Karleigh is not bad looking, either," Nick joked.

Grant turned to Nick and laughed, "I doubt we are talking about the same woman."

"Probably not." Nick patted Grant on the shoulder and returned to take more pictures.

Once the photographer was done with the wedding party, Karmyn walked toward the rear of the church. She was moving at a fast clip, and it was difficult for Nick to catch up to her. Before he could get her attention, she ran into the ladies' restroom. He waited for her to come out, but after 15 minutes, he thought something was wrong and headed in after her. No wonder the door to the ladies' room was always closed. It smelled fresh and fragrant in there as opposed to the smell of the men's room. That must be why the door to the men's room was always open, to air the place out.

"Karmyn, are you okay?" He asked, not advancing too far into the room.

"Nick? Why are you in here?" Karmyn asked from behind a closed bathroom stall.

"I saw you come in, and you've been in here for a while. I was just checking on you."

"Well, I'm fine. You can leave now."

Nick didn't want to leave her alone. He sensed she needed someone to talk to. This feeling of wanting to be there for her was foreign to him. No other woman he had been involved with had evoked this emotion from him. Before Karmyn, he would not have cared if a woman had walked away from him. There were too many fish in the sea. But this time, there was only one fish that grabbed his hook.

"Ok, I'll wait for you outside," Nick said as he went to walk away.

"No!" Karmyn yelled. "Don't wait for me. You can leave. I'll meet you at the reception."

There was a well-planned entrance dance that all of the wedding attendants had choreographed. There was about an hour before the wedding party needed to be at the reception. But he was in no way leaving without making sure Karmyn was okay.

"OK, I'll wait for you." He repeated himself, hoping she understood he wasn't leaving.

He heard her angrily sigh before he closed the door. Nick was not getting any good guy points from Karmyn today, but he didn't care. Her well-being was his immediate concern.

He waited outside until she exited the restroom. Karmyn tried to walk away in the opposite direction, but Nick blocked her path.

"Why did you wait? I told you to leave," Karmyn asked, clearly frustrated that he was still there.

"And I told you I was waiting." Nick stared at her intently. "I wanted to make sure you were okay."

"Well, I am, thanks." She attempted to step around him. Nick moved to the side right with her.

"What's wrong with you?" Nick reached for her hand. Karmyn gave him a quick karate chop to the throat and swirled around, throwing Nick off-balance when she made contact. He instantly went for his throat, and she came back with a jab to the side.

"Are you crazy?" Nick asked with bated breath. He was kneeling over in a fair amount of pain.

"Leave me alone," she screamed and tried to walk away again.

Nick was getting angrier. He had no idea what had changed between them since earlier in the day, but he was determined to find out. Trying again, he grabbed both arms this time.

"Stop, talk to me," he pleaded with her.

There was a fire in her eyes, and before he could react, she stomped on his foot and tried to knee him in the family jewels. Nick released her in enough time to protect himself.

"Stay away from me! I hate you," Karmyn yelled.

"You're neurotic!" Nick yelled, matching her temper. "Bipolar or something. Get some counseling," he stormed off in the opposite direction.

Nick had no idea what was going on with Karmyn. She didn't even behave that way when they bumped into each other in the government building. Karmyn had been cordial at the coffee shop, and earlier today, she seemed fine during the wedding. Then all of a sudden, she snapped and became this neurotic princess.

"Nick, what's going on? We just saw Karmyn leave the church in tears," Simon asked him.

"What can I say? The woman is crazy." He explained to Simon what had happened. Simon simply nodded.

"What aren't you telling me," Nick asked.

"The sisters think she has the hots for someone and is having an internal struggle with it all."

Nick softened a little, hoping that her internal struggle was like his and for him. But that still didn't explain why she assaulted him. Admittedly, he may have been a tad bit aggressive, but it didn't warrant a gut punch and throat check.

"Nick, give her some time. She may be dealing with more than we know. She has never been open about her marriage or divorce from Vincent. I know you were his attorney, so you probably know more about her marriage than her sisters."

"That's just it. I probably know less." Nick had recently told Simon about the day in her attorney's office. There was something that both Karmyn and Vincent were hiding. He couldn't shake the feeling that they were both hiding something.

Once they all arrived at the reception, Karmyn asked Dallas to switch places with Nick for the introductions, entrance, and dance. As Simon suggested, he didn't question her request because he needed to give her time and space. Instead of pressing the issue, he kept his distance from her for most of the evening.

No matter what she did, Nick watched Karmyn. She was doing a good job of ignoring him and purposefully putting as much distance as possible between them. Nick didn't like it, but he would respect it for now.

Chapter 6

Karmyn hated thinking about what happened at the church after her sister's wedding. She remembered taking pictures and going to the restroom. Then she was punching Nick in the throat. After that, she was so embarrassed at what transpired she ran from the church in tears. Instead of riding back to the hotel with the wedding party, she walked for a few blocks before calling for an Uber. Being around anyone at that moment would probably cause her to have a mental break.

What she did was deplorable, and she needed to apologize to Nick. She didn't even know why she attacked him in that way. The throat punch was a reflex. The knee to the groin that he blocked was more personal. She didn't want to be attracted to him, yet she was fighting that attraction within.

When she arrived at the reception, she immediately notified the wedding coordinator there was a switch with the wedding party and introductions. Once the remaining wedding party arrived, the change had been made. She didn't care that Nick looked angry about it. That was his problem. Being near him was causing issues to her mental health, and she needed the distance.

The reception was beautiful, and Karmyn couldn't be happier for her sister. Karleigh deserved all of the happiness that life had to offer. The love that Karleigh and Simon shared was evident in the way they looked at each other.

Karmyn still hoped to one day fight her demons and find love again. And when she did, she hoped he was just like Simon. While she watched the newly wedded couple enjoy their last dance, she sensed Nick approaching her. Karmyn quickly stepped away from the dance floor and exited through a crowd of people, hoping that Nick didn't follow her.

She was grateful when Simon, Nick, and their fraternity brothers started doing their fraternity stroll around the dance floor, allowing Karleigh to slip out of the room and change into her third wedding dress for the evening. Karmyn was happy to assist her sister into another dress. It gave her a reason to retreat from the reception. In the bridal dressing room, she helped Karleigh get dressed.

"What's wrong, Sister?" Karleigh asked while Karmyn buttoned the back of the dress.

"Nothing. Why do you ask?" Karmyn nonchalantly responded.

"Don't do that. I saw you leaving the church, and I noticed you changed the lineup for the reception entrance. I didn't know you hated Nick that much. You two had been very cordial throughout the planning process."

"I don't hate him. I just don't trust myself around him," Karmyn admitted. It was time she shared the truth about her and Nick with her sister. Holding it in had taken its toll on her, and maybe that was why she had the short mental break earlier.

"You don't trust yourself around who?" Poe asked when she entered the room.

"Nick. He was Vincent's attorney during the divorce."

Both sisters said, "Ohh," like that explained everything. Then, both said, "ooohh," finally realizing that Nick was the man she found herself attracted to.

"Yeah, well, that's just the beginning of things," Karmyn told her sisters what transpired since the elevator incident, including her nightly dreams of the handsome attorney.

"Okay, let me make sure I have it. Nick called you a gold-digger and tried to convince Vincent not to give in to your divorce request, even though it was spelled out in the pre-nuptial agreement. Then, you bump into each other at Karleigh's salon. For the past few months, you have had to be near him due to this wedding. Recently, you were stuck in an elevator with him, and now you are attracted to him." Poe started fanning herself with her hands. "Sister, you have some story to tell."

What the sisters didn't know was her feelings were increasing each time they were near. And now she needed his help and was considering accepting his trip proposal. Lord knows she needed a vacation, just not with him. A weekend in his presence, partying, even if it was for his parent's anniversary, was too close for comfort.

The sisters talked about the reception as they were helping Karleigh into her going-away attire. Simon had invited a ton of the city's hot-shots and bigwigs to the wedding. His clientele was quite impressive. The current dress was Karleigh's third and final dress of the evening. The white gauze dress reminded you of summer and flowed effortlessly in the wind.

After Karleigh and Simon's send-off, Karmyn returned to the hotel suite to gather her belongings. She was thankful that she didn't run into Nick on her way out. She had contemplated getting a room in the hotel for the night just to avoid running into him. But that was childish, and instead, she went straight home.

Home, for Karmyn, was the loneliest place to be. But in her bedroom, she found solace. Karmyn didn't use the master bedroom in the house. It was the room she shared with Vincent. After the divorce was finalized, she emptied the space of all its furniture and left it bare. She opted to sleep in a smaller bedroom that had windows that overlooked the wooded backyard. Karmyn enjoyed waking to the sunrise and seeing the deer cross her yard when the sun set.

She just needed to be alone to rest and reset.

Monday, after the wedding, Karmyn was in her main office when she received a package sent by courier. The envelope contained legal documents. Mr. Haney had indeed filed a lawsuit against her and the gym for negligence. One document stated that the gym had incompetent staff. Another mentioned her specifically for not providing immediate and adequate care after injury.

Karmyn hadn't expected the day to be perfect, but these accusations got her blood boiling. She called around the city looking for an attorney to represent her, but the available ones heard her name and tried to charge her an exorbitant rate. Trium-Fit Gyms were very well known among the city's elite. Unfortunately, her divorce attorney didn't handle business matters.

Unable to find any attorney to assist her, she had no choice but to call Nick. He had offered his services for free or rather a minimal cost. Karmyn wondered if she could broker a deal with him that didn't include her going out of town with him.

She called his private number instead of his office, hoping to leave a message. She hadn't expected him to answer early on a Monday morning.

"Nick Butler," he answered. The sound of his voice caused her to pause and revel in the deeply male sound. Karmyn jumped when he repeated his name.

Wanting to keep it strictly professional, she said, "Mr. Butler, this is Ms. Karmyn Hammond. It seems that I require your legal services," she fought to say while holding her anger inside.

"Ms. Hammond, I hoped you would call. It seems as though Mr. Haney's representation assumed I was representing you, and I have received the lawsuit he intends to file. He is seeking an advantageous settlement."

Karmyn hated to admit that she enjoyed the sound of his voice. It was deep and warm. He was using his professional voice because his tone with her at Karleigh's wedding was downright sensuous. That was part of the reason why she ran to the bathroom after the pictures were taken. She couldn't very well stand the thought of being next to Nick and having the feelings she was feeling. However, she still didn't understand why she reacted so harshly and angrily with him when he approached.

"Well, it seems that you are my last hope," she paused.

Gathering her thoughts before continuing, she said, "Please forgive me for my actions at the wedding. I don't know what came over me." Karmyn had to apologize. If she hadn't, the thought that she attacked him with no provocation would stay with her until she did apologize.

"Ms. Hammond, I will forgive you and take on your case as long as you accompany me to Savannah."

Karmyn rolled her eyes and glared at him through the phone. He couldn't see her, but she frowned anyway. Why was he doing this to her? She needed his help, and he was using her dilemma against her. A gentleman would never do such a thing. Then again, Nick was no gentleman.

"That is something else I want to speak with you about. Can we come to another agreement? I don't think it's right that I pretend to be your date at your parent's anniversary party. "

"On the contrary, Ms. Hammond. I believe you to be the perfect date. Besides, you will be doing me a huge favor, just as I am doing one for you."

And there it was. The idea that Nick didn't have to help her out. He could charge her the same inflated fees that all of the other attorneys were charging. But he was offering her an alternative offer that wouldn't break the bank. It would just be problematic for her sanity.

"That is low, Nick, even for you. I could always keep looking for another attorney who won't blackmail me."

"That is your choice. Let me know how that turns out for you. Good day, Ms. Hammond."

Karmyn looked at her phone, unbelieving that Nick disconnected the call. How dare he hang up on her. She was furious now. He had her pinned down, and she had to accept that she had already called every attorney in the area. She had even called attorneys in other cities, and they either declined or wanted too much money upfront.

Reaching into her desk drawer to grab an aspirin, she knew what needed to be done. The call went straight to voicemail.

Karmyn groaned because he was playing a game with her. She hated games, especially these types. She left a quick message agreeing to his request, then tried to force herself into relaxation.

She repeated her mantra over and over again. *God wouldn't bring you to it if he didn't plan to bring you through it.*

Using her fingertips to massage her temples and attempt to ease away the building migraine, she kept repeating the words. Then she remembered her grandmother once telling her not to try and understand what God had planned. No matter what it was, He had a reason for it.

A soft knock on Karmyn's office door interrupted her peace. She opened her eyes to find one of the gym's trainers in the doorway.

"Hey Karmyn, there is a guy out front, in a suit asking for you. I think I have seen him before."

"I'll be right there."

Karmyn counted backward from ten, pasted on a fake smile, and left her office to face probably another crisis. Her heart did a little flutter when she saw the last person in the world she wanted to see. Vincent was standing by the juice bar, chatting it up with one of the female trainers. She hadn't seen him in months and was angry by the reaction her body had to him. He was still attractive, in a rugged, schoolboy kind of way, and he always seemed larger than life.

Why was he in her place of business? What reason would Vincent have for seeking her out at this time? He had not tried to contact her since the divorce was finalized. Last she heard, he had moved cross country with one of his flings. Not wanting him in her gym any longer than necessary, she walked over to him.

"How can I help you?" Karmyn asked in her most professional tone.

"Come on, Karmyn. Why so formal?" Vincent winked at the trainer, who smiled at him. When she saw the expression that Karmyn was giving her, the trainer expeditiously walked away.

"You are in my space. What did you expect? That I would throw my arms around you? Hug you for old times' sake?" Karmyn said in a low voice so no one could hear her.

"Actually, yes. It's been a while. How have you been?" Vincent reached in for a hug, but Karmyn stepped back. She didn't want to make small talk with him. She also didn't want her personal business to be plastered in the media.

"How can I help you?" she returned to her business voice.

"Ok, that's how you want it. I'm looking for a facility to start my rehab. I am going in for knee surgery in a few weeks. Your *place of business* is being tossed around as the best place for athletes to get physical therapy."

Great, that was all she needed was to have Vincent lurking around all the time. Especially when Karmyn couldn't understand why she reacted to him the way she did, she couldn't possibly still have feelings for him. He broke her heart repeatedly. Recovering from that time in her life was dark. She never wanted to feel that way again.

"Our physical therapists have an office over there," Karmyn motioned in that direction. "You are welcomed to speak with any of them. They are all great to work with. If you will excuse me, I have a client coming in." She walked away without giving him a chance to say anything. Suddenly, she felt like the walls were closing in on her, and she needed to get out of there. She grabbed her keys from her desk and quickly made her way to her car.

Karmyn started driving with no real destination and somehow ended up at Karleigh's salon again. She noticed Karleigh's car was missing, but she didn't care. The salon, in a strange way, was therapeutic.

Echo and Whisper were the only two stylists working. Karmyn decided to sit and listen to their tirades, calming herself down. If she could figure out why she had these emotional reactions, then maybe she would be able to figure out a solution.

"Hey girl, your sister just left, but she'll be back soon. You can wait in her chair." Echo told her.

"Thanks, Echo."

Whisper was at the shampoo bowl attending to one of her clients. "Is everything alright, Karmyn?" she asked.

"I'll be okay." Karmyn sat in her sister's stylist chair and dropped her head down. She felt exposed, even though no one in the salon knew what she was dealing with.

"You know, talking things out sometimes helps you to identify your feelings," Whisper offered.

"Who are you now, Dr. Phil? Iyanla? Yes, beloved." The ladies in the salon laughed at Echo's impression of Iyanla Vanzant.

"I'm just saying, talking is sometimes helpful." Whisper grabbed a towel and wrapped it around her client's neck before walking with her back to her styling station.

Karmyn agreed with Whisper. The sole reason she came to the salon was to talk with other women. They often had viewpoints and perspectives that Karmyn didn't think to consider. Their advice was hit or miss but is always given in sisterhood, friendship, and love.

"Okay, so you all know who my ex-husband is. Well, he came into my gym today. He said he was going to need physical therapy services in a few weeks after knee surgery. Of all the physical therapists in the city, why come to mine?"

The salon was quiet for a few seconds. Only the sound of the music in the background could be heard. Mrs. Lang, an older lady and client of Whisper, spoke up first. "Are the other therapists better than yours?"

Karmyn thought about her answer before speaking. There was nothing special about her therapists. One could say they might be better because they specialize in athletes recovering from injury. But, many other physical therapist offices did the same. "I would say they are about the same. I offer add-on services in my gym specific to athletes."

"And your ex-husband is an athlete, right?" Mrs. Lang asked.

"Right," Karmyn responded, not knowing where Mrs. Lang was

going with her line of questioning.

"Uh-huh." Mrs. Lang turned back to the magazine she had been reading.

"What Mrs. Lang is saying is…," Echo tried to clarify.

Mrs. Lang jumped right in, "She ain't stupid. She heard what I said."

The customers and stylists remained quiet. Karmyn was left to read between the lines. She did offer a unique service for athletes, which was the draw for them to patronize her business. Maybe she was overthinking things with Vincent. Yet, the real issue was with the reaction she had to see him. That was something she would not share with these ladies and possibly not even her sisters.

The ladies' conversation moved on to something new, and Karmyn realized she still had not heard from Nick about handling her case. After leaving the salon, she drove over to Nick's office. When she arrived, there was a moving truck and several men packing crates. There was also a lady barking orders inside of the office. She was wearing jeans and a polo shirt, but she seemed to be in charge. Karmyn assumed she was the office manager or someone like that.

"Excuse me. I'm looking for Mr. Butler," Karmyn asked once she was able to get the woman's attention.

Not giving her a second glance, the woman answered, "He went over to the new location. We will be closed for the remainder of this week as we transition."

"He and I talked earlier today. Where is the new location?"

The lady hesitated before giving her the address. "It's in the Roget's Tower. You may find Mr. Butler over there."

Karmyn knew the address and the building very well. It was the same building where her gym and primary office were located. She turned and stalked away before the lady could see the steam rising from her ears. Nick was manipulative and downright conniving. How dare he move into her building.

It wasn't that she owned the building; there were several other business offices located there. But he could have at least given her a heads up. She pondered whether he was doing this on purpose. Moving into her building would cause them to see each other every day possibly.

Traffic was light on her way back to the gym, arriving in just under 20 minutes. Karmyn was grateful for the assigned parking spaces that came with a lease in the Roget's building. Parking in the area was sometimes treacherous. She noticed Nick's sports car parked five spots over. Seeing it there solidified that Nick was indeed in her building. She was silently hoping the woman had given her the wrong address.

When Karmyn entered her gym, one of her new trainers was coming toward her. She didn't have time to deal with any member issues at the time. The new trainer was young and fresh from college with a degree in kinesiology. Karmyn liked the young girl's attitude and unique ideas for training. She also had tons of questions about handling members. But right now, wasn't the time for dealing with her.

"Ms. Hammond. Uh, Ms. Hammond?"

"I don't have the time right now. Can you talk to Richard or Cassie?"

"I don't have a question. I just need to tell you…."

Cutting her off, Karmyn kept walking toward her office. "Can it wait until later? I'm swamped right now." Karmyn entered her office and saw Nick comfortably sitting in a chair across from her desk, reading something on his phone. "What are you doing in my office?"

"That's what I wanted to tell you. Mr. Butler was waiting for you."

"Thanks," Karmyn nodded to the young woman.

"You couldn't just call me." Karmyn stood beside her desk. She was still fuming about the idea that he would be so close daily. She thought about moving her office to another location on the drive over but quickly nixed that idea. She was in this building first.

"Since I was in the building, I thought I would stop by," Nick stood and adjusted his suit jacket.

Karmyn didn't want him to know how much his action affected her. She swallowed hard before walking around her desk to take a seat. "Really. And you couldn't tell me that you were moving into my building?"

"I tried to tell you last week when I stopped by. But you were busy with Mr. Haney. By the way, I took the liberty of filing a motion to dismiss his lawsuit. His claims are frivolous, and he will just be wasting money if he continues. He has until the end of the month to drop the case."

"That's fine with me," Karmyn released a frustrated breath.

"I had another reason to stop by. The anniversary party is next week. I hate that I used my parents as a way to get you to come with me. But I need your help. My mom will parade women before me, and I don't want to deal with it. If you are there with me, I know I can enjoy my visit home."

If Karmyn kept this trip strictly on a friendship level and not read too much into it, then maybe she would be able to handle being near Nick for an entire weekend. She did need a vacation, and he was offering her a free trip to Savannah. "I need a break anyway. You need me to block for you, and I need a vacation. I guess we are going to Savannah."

Nick audibly sighed, releasing the breath he was holding. Karmyn smiled at the knowledge that he was nervous about asking her again.

*****

Nick's assistant emailed Karmyn the itinerary for her travel. She was going to arrive on Friday and return on Sunday afternoon. There was no reason she needed to be there for the entire week. He just needed her for the main events.

His parents planned several dinner parties for different groups of friends and a big soiree on Friday night. There was also a huge family and friends picnic on Saturday and a spectacular Sunday service at the church where they were married.

When his parents got married, many family and friends told them they would never make it. His dad barely graduated from high school and was working at the shipyards in Savannah when they met. His mother was a student at Savannah State University and came from a wealthy family. His mother's family didn't approve of the two of them dating. They thought she deserved someone from a wealthy family like theirs. And when they decided to marry against her parent's wishes, her family cut her off.

Eventually, her family came around once Nick was born. His grandparents wanted nothing but to be in their grandchildren's lives. They accepted Virgil Butler only because he was the father of their grandchild. They never knew how much money he saved living a simple life and how much he was worth due to investments he learned about while working with guys on the docks.

Nick thought about his parents, his brothers, and his other family members. They were all good people and successful in their chosen career fields. The Butler family had doctors, lawyers, an award-winning journalist, and a crazy successful travel agent. His cousin Patty made millions of dollars sending large groups on faraway travel excursions.

Thinking about all of their accomplishments made Nick smile. Even though they were considered wealthy, they were a regular down-to-earth family. Only Nick and his brothers were flashy with their success. For Nick, it was because of his clientele, they expected it. His brothers were just young and full of themselves.

Nigel and Nathan had been told they were handsome since they were in elementary school. The girls fed into their egos in high school. By the time they went to college, it was too late. All three brothers had been asked if they were models, actors, or athletes at some point in their lives. Nick grew tired of it quickly; Nigel and Nathan still enjoyed the attention.

"Nick, the car service is here," his assistant announced, interrupting his thoughts.

In two days, Nick would be spending a weekend with the woman who occupied his dreams. He hoped he was ready for it. His intention was not to woo or seduce her but rather to get to know one another as friends.

The flight to Savannah was smooth and uneventful. Thankful for that, he gathered his carry-on belongings and exited the aircraft. Nick wasn't shocked that his brother Nathan was there to pick him up, and he wasn't surprised that he somehow made it through the TSA checkpoint without an airline ticket.

"Do I even need to ask?" Nick started shaking his head at his brother's antics.

"Monica works for TSA. She always hooks me up," Nathan answered, reaching for his brother's carry-on bag.

"And Monica is?" Nick asked, handing his bag to his brother.

"Don't worry about it," Nathan laughed.

On the ride to their parent's house on Tybee Island, Nathan filled him in on his career and current cases. Nathan chose to go into corporate law, while Nigel preferred civil rights law and currently worked for the Innocence Project–an organization dedicated to exonerating wrongfully convicted people through DNA testing and reforming the criminal justice system.

Both of his brothers lived in Washington D.C., and Nick wouldn't be surprised if Nigel planned to run for an elected office in his future. He was the brother who had always been interested in politics.

Nick saw the house he bought for his parents appear through the trees. An overwhelming, calming feeling washed over his body when the car came to a stop. He was home. It wasn't the home he was raised in, but it still felt good. It had been years since he had been there, preferring for his family to visit him. Nick had no real reason for staying away so long.

The most loving and understanding woman was standing on the steps wearing a huge smile that brightened Nick's day.

"My firstborn baby," his mother cried.

"Mom, I missed you." Nick wrapped his arms around her and pulled her into a bear hug. He lifted her off her feet and kissed her cheek. He gently placed her back on the ground. "How's my favorite girl?"

"Wishing you would find a new favorite girl. What is this I hear about you having a plus one this week?" She swatted him with the towel then put her hands on her hips. The look that said, *"you better tell me the truth."*

He had not been in her presence for 30 seconds before she started with the inquisition. The questions were always about his lack of a woman in his life. Dorothy Butler wanted daughters and grandchildren. The only daughters would have to be daughters-in-law.

"Mom, let the boy in the house before you start with the interrogation," Nathan joked.

"Nathan, don't think I have forgotten about you. I ought to box your ears off," his mother threatened in a joking manner.

"What did Nate do?" Nick felt like he was left out of an inside joke.

"Never you mind. You just tell me about this young lady. It must be serious if you are bringing her around the family." Dorothy looped her arm through Nick's and walked him toward the house.

"Mom, you will have to wait until she gets here on Friday," Nick gave her his signature smile that melted women's hearts.

Nick kissed his mother again and took off through the house, looking for his father. It was a short search because Virgil was exactly where Nick expected him to be. His father was sitting in front of his obnoxiously large television, reading a magazine with the volume on mute.

"Father, why do you insist on having the television on with no sound?" Nick asked.

"Gives me something to look at when your mother is in another room." His father stretched to his full 6'6" height, then looked his son over from head to toe before grabbing him in the same bear hug he had just given his mother.

"Looking good, kid. Not as good as me, but you'll do," his father laughed. People usually thought they were brothers instead of father and son whenever the Butler men were out together. Another nod to their excellent gene pool.

"If we are talking about looks, I'm the best looking one of all," Nigel said as he entered the room with Nathan on his heels.

"Why am I not surprised by that response," Nick laughed and hugged his brother.

"What can I say? The ladies love me." Nigel was the more arrogant brother.

"Well, I wish *you* loved you less," Nick teased Nigel.

Dorothy entered the room to announce, "Men, I have lunch in the kitchen. Dinner is promptly at 6 pm tonight. Suits with jackets and ties are to be worn. Tonight's dinner is with a few of my sorority sisters and their spouses. And sons, absolutely no lawyer talk at the dinner table. I don't care if my guests bring it up first."

The first night's dinner party was pleasant. There was no lawyer talk among the brothers, and no single women were in attendance. Nick was pleasantly surprised. Maybe his mother had taken the hint that he had an interest in someone else. However, that was not the case at the second dinner party.

The next evening, the dinner party included distinguished alumni from Savannah State University, including the school president and his daughter, a recent Florida A&M Pharmacy school graduate. Madelyn was a beautiful woman. Probably someone Nick would date had he not had his eyes on another beauty who owned a fitness gym. Nathan and Nigel were eyeing the young pharmacist, but neither engaged her in conversation. They didn't want to encourage their mother in her match-making ways.

"My Nicolas is also a fellow rattler. I would have preferred he go to Savannah State, but we can't always get what we wish for," his mother laughed. She was always gushing about her boys but was secretly saddened that none attended her alma mater.

Madelyn leaned toward Nick and whispered, "I can tell you are uncomfortable with your mother presenting women to you. It's written all over your face. My mother has been doing the same thing to me since I graduated." They shared a quick laugh.

Nick faced the same fate the next night when the dinner party included the neighbors. Since they lived in a gated community, the neighbors walked over for a luau-styled festive barbecue. No suits were required. Somehow Nathan and Nigel escaped the barrage of women being thrust in front of him. Every once in a while, Nick would see his brothers standing away from the crowd laughing at him.

After turning down, yet another invitation for lunch or dinner with a single woman, Nick made his way to his brothers.

"So, tell me how you two are not included in tonight's episode of who wants to date a millionaire?"

"First, we are not yet millionaires. Second, mom can only focus on one son at a time."

"And you are the oldest," Nigel laughed before taking a sip of his beer.

Nick wanted to stop his mother from her shenanigans, but he was sure it wouldn't matter to her. He found out she suspected that his inviting a date was a ploy to stop her. That is why she did not stop parading single women in front of him. He just hoped she would stop once Karmyn arrived. That would be rude and disrespectful, even if they weren't dating.

Nick was on pins as he awaited Karmyn's flight to land. He was able to use Nathan's friend Monica to allow him past the security checkpoint. Nick felt like a fool waiting for her to appear with a bouquet of pink and yellow roses in hand. She should have been one of the first people off the plane since he ensured she was seated in first class. He was confused when she finally appeared after the majority of the people had disembarked.

"Nice flowers," she said as she approached him.

"Why are you so far back?" Nick asked.

"Well, there was a seating change. There was a mother and her infant whom I thought needed the space more than I did, so I switched with her."

Nick shook his head and laughed. His laughter grew to a roar as he thought about the situation. Of course, she would give up her first-class seat to someone who would benefit from it. That was her style.

"Did I say something funny?" Karmyn asked.

"I was just thinking how different you are from…." He didn't finish his statement because Karmyn would undoubtedly bring up his initial thoughts of her character during her divorce. But he did not know her then, and he had made an offensive assumption about her.

"Never mind. These flowers are for you. And you are looking exceptionally beautiful today."

She traded him her carry-on suitcase for the flowers. Together they exited the terminal and headed for the parking lot. When they stopped at the black Bugatti, Karmyn paused then gave Nick a questioning look.

"This is not my car. My brother likes flashy things, and this car is just one of them. You will understand when you meet him." Nick opened the door for Karmyn, allowing her to get in and get comfortable. He placed her bag in the rear and slid into the driver's seat.

Karmyn reached over and grabbed Nick's hand, stopping him from putting the car into gear. The touch was electric, and he felt the tingle shoot straight up his arm. She was intentionally touching him, and it wasn't a defensive move or a karate chop.

"Promise me you will stay within the speed limit? I know this car can get up to 400 miles per hour," Karmyn smiled.

Her smile took Nick to another place. A place where they were really a couple and enjoying life together. Returning her smile, "I promise you, we will never find out if this car goes that fast."

They traveled in silence from the airport to the island. A few times, Nick looked over at Karmyn and smiled at how she stared out of the window like a true tourist. She had told him she had never visited the area before, and he looked forward to taking her sightseeing.

When they arrived at his parents' house, Karmyn's jaw dropped in awe of the home.

"You grew up here?" she asked in stunned disbelief.

"No. I bought this house for my parents when I landed my first celebrity client. It was a wreck, but after a year of sweat labor, blood, and tears, my brothers and I were able to restore it to this beauty."

"You did the renovation yourself? I can't picture it."

"Looks can be deceiving, right?"

Nick retrieved her bag from the back and escorted her into the house. Amazingly, his mother was not the waiting welcome wagon like before. He expected her to be on the steps waiting to meet the only woman he had willingly invited to his parents' home.

They entered the kitchen and walked into a ridiculous discussion that bordered on an argument between his mother and Nathan. His mother was preparing lunch while Nathan was pleading his case.

"What is going on in here?" Nick interrupted.

"Mother here wants me to escort one of her sorority sisters to the dinner tonight and all weekend," Nathan angrily answered.

"Mom, he's a little young for one of your sorors, isn't he?" Nick was trying to lighten the mood. He didn't want Karmyn's first impression of his family to be a negative one.

Dorothy slammed the knife down that she had been using to chop vegetables onto the kitchen counter. "What a ridiculous statement to make, Nicolas. She is only 22 years old and a recent graduate of Georgia Southern University. I was mentoring her during her senior year, and I want her to attend the events for the weekend. She won't know anyone. Between Nathan and Nigel,

Nathan is the most honorable."

She had a point. Nigel was a skirt-chaser of the worst kind. He wouldn't give it a second thought to take the woman home and entertain her. Nathan, on the other hand, was very selective about the women he spent his time with. "Well, brother, she has you there. Nigel would be trying to take her home," Nick said.

"This is not fair. I'll do it, but remember it is under duress." Nathan stormed from the kitchen.

Nick laughed at his brother's dramatic exit. Nathan would probably calm down after he met the woman. If she were attractive, his anger would lessen even more. He turned to Karmyn, "I'm sorry you had to see that." Nick then made the introductions.

"It's a pleasure to meet you, Mrs. Butler, and happy anniversary." Karmyn nervously shifted from one foot to the other.

"Thank you, sweetheart, and call me Dottie." She gave Karmyn the once over. "You know, I didn't think you were real. Nicolas has never willingly let me meet any woman he has truly been interested in since high school. I have had to get creative to meet his dates. Even the ones from law school." She winked at Nick, who responded by rolling his eyes upward.

Nick loved his mother. Over the years, when he dated someone, he wanted to wait a while before introducing her to the family. His mother had a gift for seeing character flaws in people that no one else saw.

Dottie wasn't kidding when she mentioned being creative in meeting the women in Nick's life. Once, she paid $500 for a charity ball ticket just to meet his date. Immediately after meeting his mother, his date labeled him a mama's boy and never called him again. Dottie simply said, "She wasn't the one, anyway."

"That's because I haven't truly been interested in anyone until now." Nick flashed that signature smile at Karmyn.

Dottie smiled then continued, "Well, I just assumed he told me he had a plus one, so I wouldn't... Well, never mind that. Are you hungry, Karmyn? I was just preparing lunch." She turned away from the couple and reached into the refrigerator, looking for another item.

"No, thank you. I had a hearty breakfast," Karmyn replied.

"Well, there are cold cuts in the refrigerator, just in case." Dottie started rinsing more vegetables in the sink. She turned to Nick. "Nicolas, show her to her room and let her relax. Dinner tonight begins at 7 pm promptly. The car service will be here at 6 pm. I look forward to seeing you both later."

His mother gave both of them a once over and continued with her food preparation.

Nicolas tried to measure Karmyn's mood after meeting his mother and briefly seeing his brother. She didn't seem to be affected by either. He was relieved that neither of their antics dissuaded Karmyn in any way. At least he hoped they didn't. Nick wanted to show off his family to Karmyn. He was very proud of them, especially his brothers.

"Come on, let me show you to your room. My mother put you in a guest room in the main house. There is also a guest house just off the pool in the back with two bedrooms where my brothers and I will be. I guess my mother wanted you close by to her. She didn't want me to sneak into your room in the middle of the night." Nick laughed at Karmyn's expression of indifference.

After showing Karmyn to her room, Nick gave her a tour of the house. They ended the tour at the pool where his brothers were lounging. They had taken a swim and were now resting.

"Karmyn, these are my knuckleheaded brothers. You remember Nathan from earlier. The ugly one is Nigel," Nick introduced them.

"I'm far from ugly." Nigel stood to greet Karmyn properly by holding her hand then leaning in for a hug. The hug lingered longer than Nick wanted and pulled Karmyn from Nigel's embrace.

"Don't be jealous, Nick. The lady will decide," Nathan gave her a wink.

"Decide what?" Karmyn looked back and forth between the

brothers.

"If I'm the ugly brother or if Nick is just jealous that I look better than him."

"Oh! I see it now," Karmyn said with a huge grin. "This is the brother with the Bugatti?"

Nick and Nathan couldn't contain their laughter. At the same time, Nigel bent over and reached for the ground, imitating picking up his broken face and putting back in place. Nigel's theatrics caused Karmyn to let go of herself a little and start laughing.

Nick liked the way she smiled when she laughed. He noticed the crinkle near her eyes and how her smile brightened more than he had ever seen. She was a beautiful woman, and Nick felt honored that she was there with him.

An awkward silence overcame them. Nick saw his brothers giving him an odd look right when Karmyn noticed. Before the brothers could speak, Karmyn excused herself, "I think I will partake of those cold cuts your mother mentioned and go to my room. I will probably take a nap for an hour before I need to start getting ready. Nice to meet you two."

The brothers mumbled "later" as Karmyn walked away.

"Nick, are you sure about her? She is the total opposite of the women I have seen you with," Nigel asked after Karmyn had entered the house.

"Yeah, this one seems smart and not pretentious," Nathan added.

Nick gave both his brothers a mean look he used from their childhood. It was the look that would make them both cringe and run crying to their parents. Through clenched teeth, Nick replied, "I don't have a type."

"Sure, you don't." Nathan grabbed his towel and cell phone, then turned back to Nick. "But we will have proof tonight. Mom invited some of your history to tonight's dinner."

"What do you mean by that? Who did she invite?"

Nathan and Nigel both walked away laughing without answering his question. Nick knew his mother kept in contact with a few of the women he had dated over the years, but he hadn't heard any names in a few years. He stopped bringing women around his mother when she was more friendly with them than he was.

*****

Karmyn paced the room over and over again. She was nervous about going to dinner on the arm of the man she once despised. The dress she was wearing was meant to make a statement. A beautiful black gown she borrowed from her sister Kyna. The evening dress was a form-fitting, one-shoulder designer original from Ashley Nicole. Her designs were always elegant and one of a kind.

She was waiting for Nick to arrive and escort her downstairs. As Karmyn was pacing the room, she began overthinking the entire weekend. If she could make it through the evening, maybe she could find an excuse to head home tomorrow. Her current feelings were insane. She was becoming attracted to her ex-husband's divorce attorney. But why now? Why did these feelings just begin to manifest?

The sudden knocking on the door startled Karmyn back to the present. It was showtime. The Butler family were riding together in a limousine to the anniversary dinner. His mother wanted to make a grand entrance and be presented to their guests by her sons. The whole scenario was like something from a movie.

After a few deep breaths, she was able to answer the door.

Nick was fiddling with his cufflinks when she opened the door. "What took you so… Whoa!"

"Is this too much?" Karmyn inwardly smiled at his reaction but only gave him a brief smile.

"No, you're gorgeous." Nick was staring at her with his mouth still open.

"Please don't gawk. You are making me uncomfortable."

"Sorry about that. Uh, we are just waiting on Nigel."

Karmyn watched Nick become uncomfortable. In every interaction she had with him, he was always self-assured and confident. At this moment, she was seeing a different side of the attorney to the stars. Not wanting to make the moment any more tense, Karmyn walked away from the door.

"Okay, let me grab my purse."

Karmyn's fingers were shaking as she reached for her matching sequined purse. She tried to take another breath to calm her nerves, but it wasn't working. Before she turned around, she said a quick prayer asking God to help her through the evening without making a fool of herself.

When she faced him again, she noticed how handsome he was, wearing an all-black Ralph Lauren tuxedo. The suit was tailor-made and accentuated his muscular physique. She tried not to notice how well built he was. His current attire was making that difficult. And his cologne had her woozy from thoughts she shouldn't be having.

"This way, milady," Nick offered his elbow.

She went to loop her arm through his when Nigel knocked him out of the way and offered his arm.

"Madam, I believe a woman as beautiful as you should be escorted with the more handsome brother. Please let me do the honor."

Karmyn looked back and forth between the two brothers. She wanted to laugh at the way Nick was staring at his brother with anger and discontent. The scene was comical and giving her something else to focus on other than her nerves.

"Well, Nigel, thank you, but I happen to think I was with the most handsome brother." Karmyn walked past Nigel and looped her arm in Nick's elbow. Together they descended the stairs leaving Nigel behind with his jaw wide opened.

Halfway down the steps, they heard Nigel say, "But I'm a Kappa."

Waiting at the bottom of the steps were Nathan, standing with a stunning young woman, and their parents. Dorothy and Virgil Butler were a striking couple, wearing coordinated formal attire of white and kente cloth accents.

Dottie saw the couple approach and scanned them from head to toe. "Don't you look beautiful? That gown was made for you."

"Thank you, Mrs. Butler." Karmyn ducked her head and attempted to extricate her arm from Nick, but he held tight.

"No, no, no, please call me Dottie. Is your gown designer made?"

"Yes. It's borrowed. My sister has expensive taste." Karmyn nervously responded.

"What she has is friends. I would know an Ashley Nicole design anywhere."

Karmyn blushed and gazed up to see Nick beaming down at her. In his eyes, she saw something she wasn't expecting. There was a passion in his eyes that mirrored her own.

Nigel interrupted the moment, "Well, I'm here. We can leave now."

Dottie exaggeratedly rolled her eyes. "Nigel, just once, can this night be about someone other than you."

"Mother, this evening is about the two human beings who created this perfection."

"Jesus, let's just go," Virgil opened the front door and escorted his beautiful wife outside.

The ride to the hotel was done in mostly silence. Karmyn was able to see more of the area through the window. Lots of trees everywhere, including beautiful magnolias. The limo pulled up to the JW Marriott in downtown Savannah. The hotel was located right on the river and was very beautiful.

As they entered the hotel, A young lady whisked the Butler

family away and had another hostess escort Karmyn and Robin, Nathan's date, to their table. There was a sweetheart table on the dancefloor. Karmyn assumed it was for Mr. and Mrs. Butler.

Everything in the room was beautiful. Form the large, crystal centerpieces filled with red and white roses to their initials as an ice sculpture. Even the guests milling about the room were breathtakingly gorgeous. The lights in the room began to dim, indicating that everyone should take their seats.

The music calmed to a low hum until the room was quieted and everyone was seated. Suddenly the DJ announced, "Ladies and Gentlemen, on this day, 40 years ago, two people stood before many of you, family and friends, and declared their lives to one another. For richer or poorer, in sickness and in health as long as they both shall live. Being escorted by their three sons, I present to you, Mr. and Mrs. Virgil and Dorothy Butler."

The DJ made the announcement sound like a sporting event and held out the last syllable of their last name for several seconds as he mixed in the song "Ain't No Stopping Us Now." The main doors to the ballroom opened, and the guests of honor followed right behind their sons. They weaved in and around every table, thanking their guests for attending, eventually making their way to the sweetheart table. After their parents were seated, the sons joined their dates at a table close to the dance floor.

Karmyn had never seen anything so magnificent. There were at least 100 guests; and when dinner was served, each guest had a personal server. The servers placed the domed platters on the table and uncovered the meal in unison. Simply spectacular.

"Do your parents always do things in this grand of a manner?" Karmyn asked Nick after their salad plates had been removed.

"My mom does everything over the top. Imagine what she will do for her 50th anniversary."

Nathan overheard them and added, "That will have to top this and whatever she is planning for her 75th birthday."

"Oh yeah. That's a few years away," Nick answered.

"Believe me, she is planning now," Nathan laughed before

eating a fork full of salad.

For the next 30 minutes, they ate in companionable silence. Instead of dessert being served, there was a huge dessert table with an assortment of goodies. Karmyn noticed several people were walking about the room chatting with others. She was about to ask if Nick wanted dessert when a tall, slender woman approached their table.

Karmyn, the fitness trainer, assessed the woman from head to toe and didn't think the woman was eating enough. She had no muscle mass, and the dress was practically wearing her.

"Hey Nick, when did you get back in town?" the woman placed her hand on Nick's shoulder to grab his attention.

"Hi Jasmine, I've been here all week," Nick answered her calmly. He never raised his head to look at her. Karmyn thought there definitely used to be something between the two.

"And you didn't call me. Is she the reason?" Jasmine tossed the insult with a terribly sweet voice that bordered on screeching. Karmyn thought the woman to be very bold. She stood over them and dared to turn her nose up when she looked at Karmyn.

"I don't need a reason not to call you. Pardon me; you have been rude to my guest. Have a nice evening." Nick stood, turning his back to Jasmine, and without giving her a second glance turned to Karmyn.

"Would you like some dessert?" Nick asked.

Karmyn accepted and took the arm he offered. Jasmine was still standing there, pouting like a schoolgirl. Nathan and Nigel were trying to hold their laughter and doing a terrible job at it.

"One of your ex-girlfriends?" Karmyn asked, not expecting an honest answer.

"No. More like a complete mistake." His tone meant the discussion was over. There had to be more to their mistake if he was so closed off about it. But why did she care? They were not a couple.

On their journey to the dessert table, they stopped to talk to

Nick's aunt, Heather. She was three years younger than her sister, Nick's mother. Heather didn't look a day over 50 years old.

Next, Nick introduced him to his mother's other two sisters, Joyce and Barbara. Karmyn laughed at the similarities between Nick's mother and herself. They both had three sisters and were the third oldest sister of the group.

More than once, one of the aunts mentioned how striking they looked as a couple, and to everyone, that is what they were, a couple. A few times, Karmyn found herself caught up in the fairytale. She tried dismissing the thoughts she was having of what it would be like to date Nicolas Butler. In the end, she gave in to the fantasy.

That daydream was doused with a cold breeze when two other women approached them. These two didn't appear as evil as Jasmine upon their approach. Both were attractive and not nearly as thin as Jasmine. Obvious to Karmyn, these women took care of their bodies.

"Nicolas, you finally found a woman who can stand being around you for more than five minutes?" She then turned to Karmyn, "You won't make it past 60 days."

The two women walked away laughing hysterically.

"Who was that?" Karmyn asked in her kindest voice. She was inwardly seething.

"A situation that lasted too long," he replied with finality.

"Apparently, only 60 days," Karmyn whispered under her breath. She knew Nick heard her when he tensed under her touch.

By the end of the evening, Karmyn had met four ex-girlfriends, two situations, and a few, *I wish I was his girlfriend, but I didn't get the chance*. She was exhausted, and on the ride back to the house, Karmyn stayed quiet. If she were to talk now, she might explode. Why would he bring her into this mess of his?

She was humiliated at least twice and entirely ignored on a few occasions. Trying to make it through the night without losing her religion was near impossible until Dottie caught up to her in the hallway.

"Karmyn, please forgive me."

"For what?"

"I am just a friendly person, and I never realized how many women my sons had been involved with on some level that I maintained a friendship with over the years. It had to be uncomfortable for you."

"Not to worry. I'm not easily intimidated."

"Good. I hope you enjoy the rest of the party."

Nick interrupted the silence. "I probably should have warned you about some of the women tonight, but I honestly didn't know she had invited so many…."

"Ex-girlfriends and situations," Karmyn finished the sentence for him.

Chapter 7

Karmyn awakened to the smell of burning charcoal. She quickly sat straight up in bed, confused. Was someone barbecuing at 6 am? Deciding to work off the stress of the party last evening, she dressed in her workout attire prepared for a run. Nick had informed her that twice around the community was equivalent to 1.5 miles. On most days, Karmyn ran 5-6 miles to start her day.

She eased her way downstairs to find Dottie and Virgil sitting in the kitchen. Virgil sat at the table reading a magazine while Dottie was again chopping vegetables.

"Good morning darling, going for a morning run?" Dottie asked.

"Yes, ma'am…" Karmyn corrected herself at the look Dottie gave her. "I'm sorry, Dottie. I thought I could get in a few miles of jogging before breakfast. Nick told me that I was welcomed to some fruit in your refrigerator."

"Dear, you are welcomed to anything in this house, including our son. Please, take him away." Virgil smiled, giving Karmyn a wink before returning to his magazine.

"Don't let us hold you up from your run. We can talk more when you return. I'm sure my sons will still be asleep. None of them like to rise before noon when they are not working."

Karmyn nodded and exited through the front door. She noticed a catering truck out front. Sweet Spice Caribbean Food. So that was the grill that had awakened her. Her mouth began salivating over what she hoped would be a luncheon full of flavor and tasty Caribbean treats. She would need to run twice as hard to be able to eat the way she wanted to.

The neighborhood was tranquil, with nothing but the wildlife to keep her company. Karmyn had come across a few geckos and a ton of birds on her run. The area was also full of cardinals. If you see a cardinal, it was rumored to be the soul of someone dearly departed. The only person she could think of was Vincent's mother.

Ms. Velma was a beautiful person inside and out. She had met Vincent's mother the day she came to campus to surprise her son. Only the surprise was on Ms. Velma. She found Karmyn asleep in Vincent's room. Karmyn had been sick but didn't want to miss her tutor appointment with Vincent. He was preparing for a huge test that could get him benched on the football team if he failed.

When Vincent's roommate opened the door, both boys jumped and tried to hide Karmyn lying in Vincent's bed. Karmyn didn't have the strength to move. Once Ms. Velma saw how weak Karmyn was, she decided to nurse her back to health. Ms. Velma stayed for two nights and played nurse to Karmyn and dorm mother to everyone else during her stay. She made dinner for the entire dormitory of about 100 guys for two nights.

As Karmyn ran through the neighborhood, she tried to remember the good things that happened in her marriage. Her wedding day was one of her happiest moments. The honeymoon to Bali was even better. But with every good memory came a bad one. From the nights she stayed up wondering where her husband was to the calls from strange women claiming to be his baby mama and asking her to step out of their way.

The wife of an athlete was often times brutal. She had endured so much and still hoped for the best. She had hoped for a reconciliation up until the day he finally signed the divorce papers. Even though things did not happen how she wanted them to,

Karmyn never gave up hope. Not her marriage, not on her business, and not on herself.

The run was helping her to clear her head as she wanted. After about two miles, Karmyn stopped at a bench by the lake. She sat and stared at the soft ripples of the water. They were having a calming effect on her. She would soon need to deal with the many emotions and feelings she was having. That needed to be her priority. To start, she needed to figure out her feelings for Nick.

She had hated Nick since her divorce. He made her feel inadequate and alone. Then he shows up at her sister's new hair salon. Of course, he would be her new brother-in-law's best friend. Now, he had moved his law practice into her building. This had to be some sort of evil twist to her life. What's even worse is she was in Savannah with Nick. Why would she agree to something like this? Maybe because he was footing the bill, not that she needed any money. Her gyms were doing quite well, and so were her other investments. Thanks to her father, who was a retired accountant, she had an excellent financial portfolio.

Karmyn made it back to the house, showered, and dressed without running into Nick or his brothers. She was heading down to the kitchen searching for breakfast when she heard a low whistle from behind her. She quickly turned and saw Nathan leaning against the wall.

"I think you are dating the wrong brother. You would look better walking in on my arm."

Before Karmyn could find something witty to say, Nathan grabbed her hand, placed the softest kiss on her palm, and gently tugged her toward the kitchen. When they entered together, everyone stopped and stared. She was beginning to feel awkward until Dottie approached them.

"Nathan, stay away from your brother's girlfriend. Karmyn, breakfast is on the table. We are very informal when it comes to breakfast. It's usually a grab and go."

Karmyn noticed Nick and Nigel were seated at the breakfast bar, with a plate in front of them piled high with pancakes. Virgil was sitting at the table where he was when she left for her run.

"After you have breakfast, join me outside," Dottie instructed. "I need to direct the florist and decorators. I'd love your help. Because I know none of these men will help me."

"You got that right," Nigel said right before putting a fork full of pancakes in his mouth.

"At least he said that before he put the food in his mouth." Dottie smiled and left the kitchen through the back patio doors.

The Butler family reminded her so much of her own family. From the joking around to the sheer love and pride their parents showed, the moment all felt comfortable. Karmyn looked around the kitchen and found an apple and a banana, then she grabbed a plate and grabbed four pancakes, a few pieces of bacon, and a muffin. She turned to find all three brothers staring at her.

"What?"

"You eat a lot for such a slim woman," Nigel remarked.

"I work out for a living. There are times when I indulge. This weekend is an indulgence." She blushed when she thought about what she said.

The brothers smiled but said nothing. They ate in silence for quite some time until the doorbell interrupted their peace. No one as much as blinked to answer the door.

When the doorbell rang again, Virgil looked up from his magazine. Neither brother moved. The bell rang for the third time, and Nigel stood.

"It's not even my turn to get the door," he threw over his shoulder as he stomped away from the kitchen like a small child.

"You know the rules," Nick yelled behind him.

Karmyn smiled and waited for one of them to let her in on the joke. When they didn't seem to be forthcoming, she asked.

"He was the first one to make eye contact, plus he is the youngest," Nick explained.

"How do you know he made eye contact? Neither of you looked up."

Both brothers smiled and said in unison, "we know."

Karmyn couldn't hide that she liked this side of Nick and how he interacted with his brothers. Even though they were all successful attorneys, they were like any other loving brothers. This normalized the arrogant man who once called her a gold-digger.

"Hello, Mr. Butler, Nicolas, Nathan."

The woman who entered the kitchen just ahead of Nigel was tall and beautiful. Her voice dripped with sugar until she said, Nathan. Karmyn wondered if she had some kind of past with Nathan. But that thought was nixed when she walked over to Nick and gave him a hug and kiss.

Karmyn's eyes perked up, noticing how the Butler men were all looking at her, including Nick. They were looking for her a reaction to the beauty who appeared to have ignored her when she greeted the room.

"Veronica, it's nice to see you again. This is my friend Karmyn Hammond. Karmyn, this is Veronica Chu. She is seemingly good friends with my mother," Nick said tightly through clenched teeth.

Veronica ignored Karmyn and still lingered too close to Nick. "Where is Ms. Dottie? She asked me to come over and help with the decorations. You know, my company is doing very well. We just finished decorating the guest house for Traven McMillian."

Veronica tried to name-drop to make herself seem important. Karmyn hated when women did this. To make it known, Karmyn responded, "Traven's guest house in the Hamptons? I hope you didn't change the color scheme. I really liked the Caribbean blue and sand colors. Oh, and the Chaveaux painting over the fireplace was dear to his grandmother. It has Caribbean blue colors also. I do hope you didn't touch that."

Everyone in the room, including Mr. Butler, dropped their jaw and just stared at her in disbelief. Veronica looked like she swallowed a lemon. Karmyn smiled and continued to eat her pancakes when Dottie returned to the kitchen.

"Oh, Veronica, I am glad you could make it. Have you met Karmyn?"

"We have met," Karmyn spoke first. "She was just telling me how she was hired by my friend Traven to decorate his guest house."

"Oh, well, that's nice, dear. Come on outside. We can talk out here. Karmyn, don't forget to join us after you have finished your breakfast."

* * * * *

Nick was living a moment in the twilight zone. Of all his past relationships, Veronica was the last woman he thought he would see at his parents' anniversary weekend. She didn't exactly leave a favorable impression on his parents. Nevertheless, she was here, and Karmyn was staring at him with questions. He could see the crazy ideas running through her head.

But they weren't a real couple, so why would she be giving him the death stare? He wanted to tell her Veronica was just an entanglement that lasted too long. But before he could open his mouth, his father started talking about sports.

They talked basketball and a little football. Karmyn was still quietly eating her breakfast and didn't participate in the conversation. Nick wondered if she ever talked about sports in a casual setting. Her clientele was some of the best athletes in the world. He realized name-dropping wasn't her thing, and she had only done that to Veronica because of the way she was dismissed.

Nick wanted to know what she was thinking and if she was bothered by Veronica's appearance. He had never been in a situation like this before. Rarely did he care what a woman thought if they ever bumped into a previous relationship of his. But with Karmyn, it was different. Karmyn wasn't like the other women he had dated, and that revelation bothered him the most.

Once the backyard luau party was in full swing, Nick tried

hiding away from all attendees. It seemed that his mother had invited not only Veronica but also Justine, Gianna, Terri, and Harmony. They had also been at the dinner last night.

There were over 100 people in his parents' backyard, and Nick kept running into women he would rather forget. Finally, he found a break from the crowd and slipped into his father's office. Nick was finally able to catch his breath since people began arriving. He had no idea where Karmyn was, but he was sure she was not too happy. Nick could only imagine what she must be thinking. Had he known his mother was inviting his past, he never would have suggested Karmyn accompany him.

"You hiding out too?" Nathan called out, startling Nick. He was sitting in his father's chair, with his feet atop the desk.

"I thought you were outside enjoying the festivities." Nick approached the desk and knocked Nathan's feet down.

"I was until I realized Mother is out there playing matchmaker of the worst kind. She tried to set Terri and me up on a date."

"My Terri?" Nick asked. "I doubt Mother knows we even dated. That may have been one I kept a secret."

"Yeah, well, I wouldn't want to date anyone that you have."

While the brothers were talking, the door opened, and Nigel entered.

"I knew you two would be hiding out. Why did you leave me to those sharks?"

"We thought you could handle it," Nathan laughed.

"Well, I was handling things until Angie walked in."

"My Angie?" Nathan stood up.

"Yes. And she is looking very good, but she also brought Gia with her."

Angie and Gia were best friends and dated Nathan and Nigel while in high school. The two women had plans for the brothers that neither brother wanted to be a part of.

Nick started laughing hysterically. It would be just like his mother to invite every woman the brothers had ever dated to her party. Not because she wanted them to find love, but because she was still friends with all of them. She collected friends like normal people collect keychains or shot glasses.

"Why are you laughing? Your ex-girlfriends are out there too," Nathan asked.

"Yeah, I know." Nick continued laughing.

The brothers hid out in their father's office for almost an hour before they were found. There was a soft knock on the door before Karmyn ducked her head inside.

"Your mother was right. You guys are hiding out. Too many situations and entanglements out there for you to handle?" She asked all three brothers, but her gaze landed on Nick.

Nick felt uncomfortable under her gaze. He looked around and caught the side-looks given to him from his brothers. She just didn't know the half of it. But what she thought mattered. And if he genuinely wanted anything to happen between him and her, he would need to be honest about everything upfront and not let secrets pop up later.

"I don't know about these two knuckle-heads, but yes. I can't believe my mother invited all of them," Nick proclaimed.

When Karmyn didn't respond, he asked her, "Would you please save me and stay by my side for the rest of the party? With your snappy comebacks, I think you will put half of those people in their place."

"Snappy comebacks? Well, I guess that's why I am here."

Nick thought over her statement of why she was here. Initially, he had asked her to accompany him because he knew Dottie would throw women at him every chance she had. Had he known the women would be from his past, he never would have invited Karmyn. This was not the environment he would have exposed her to.

Lately, he had been thinking of spending time with one woman, and his thoughts kept going back to Karmyn. She was everything he wanted in a woman and could never find. She was intelligent with great business sense. She was beautiful but not full of herself. Even when she was married to Vincent, she didn't live a lavish lifestyle, which says a lot about her character.

That was what he found so endearing. Karmyn had personality.

"By the way, your mother wants all three of you outside right now." Karmyn grabbed Nick's arm, "Shall we go?"

"We shall."

Chapter 8

The weekend turned out to be more enjoyable than Karmyn thought. The women they encountered at the luau were friendly and, in some cases, downright engaging to be around. Karmyn didn't need to be worried because most of Nick's ex-girlfriends were cordial. Except for Gianna and Veronica. Gianna glared and stared during the entire luncheon. Even at church service on Sunday, she couldn't stop staring.

Karmyn was grateful to be home but happy she took time off from work to get some rest. Now she was back to the grind of running her business and having to deal with Mr. Haney and his ridiculous lawsuit. That also meant she had to deal with Nick on a professional level.

She thought about the fun she had with the Butler men over the weekend when Kyna entered her office and caught her smiling.

"What's that goofy look for?" Kyna asked, taking a seat in the chair in front of Karmyn's desk.

"What goofy look?" Karmyn tried to give her sister a look of indifference but failed when she smiled again.

"Right. I just stopped by to remind you that we are meeting at Karleigh's house to help with decorations." Kyna pulled out her cell phone and started scrolling through, looking for something.

"Decorations for what?" Karmyn didn't remember any parties coming up. The wedding was over, and she thought that was enough decorating to last a few lifetimes.

"I hope you didn't forget that we volunteered to host women's day at church this year. Karleigh has decided she wants DIY decorations. I guess she didn't get enough from the wedding."

Karmyn had forgotten entirely that she volunteered for women's day and the decorating committee. It was more like being voluntold to be on the decorating committee. On top of everything else she had going on with the gym, she would also be crafting all night. She had hoped to evade her sisters for as long as possible. They would surely ask her about her weekend and want details. She wasn't ready to share with them her feelings for Nick.

"You came across town to tell me that. A text message would have done the same job." Karmyn interrupted her sister's attention to her cell phone.

Kyna wasn't the type to be on social media, so she was probably reading some medical journals or texting with her husband. That's all she seemed to do nowadays.

"You're right, but I haven't seen you since Karleigh's wedding. How are you?" Kyna dropped her phone into her handbag and focused on Karmyn.

"I guess I'm okay." Karmyn shrugged her shoulders and averted eye contact. Kyna always tried to peer into your soul when she asked questions.

"So, the little trip you took over the weekend wasn't relaxing?" Kyna sat up in her chair and leaned closer toward the desk.

Karmyn noticed her sister trying to get closer and watch her facial features. Kyna was trying to get answers to questions she didn't ask. "You have always been the nosey little sister. I relaxed a little. I'm good."

"Well, I also stopped by to check out some office space in the building. Morgan is thinking of opening an office here, and we like this area."

"Oh no! First Karleigh, then Nick, and now you. No!" Karmyn stood, placing her hands on her hips and glaring down at her sister. She used to hide out in her gym when she wanted to get away, and now her family wanting to move in was feeling smothering.

"We were just thinking about it, dang. I'll tell Morgan you said no." Kyna stood and adjusted her dress. "Fix your attitude before tonight, and I'll see you later."

Karmyn dropped back into her chair when Kyna left. Her attitude was all Nick's fault. He had her head in a tizzy. She didn't know what to do about it. She dropped her head into her hands and closed her eyes. Taking deep breaths, she tried to calm her nerves and prevent the headache that was beginning to form.

There was a knock on her door.

"Kyna, can you just call me later?"

"Looks like you need one of my special massages."

The voice was unmistakable. As if things couldn't get any worse, why was Vincent in her office? Where were the front desk people? They knew better than to let people roam around the offices, which sat in the back of the gym facilities.

"What do you want?" Karmyn asked without lifting her head to see him.

"My surgery is Thursday. And I want to rehab and do my physical therapy here."

Vincent came fully into her office and sat on the edge of her desk. His cologne was a Ralph Lauren original she bought him for his birthday a few years ago. She loved the way it smelled on him. Even now, the fragrance was wreaking havoc on her senses. Instead of standing or looking up at him, she remained seated behind her desk, still rubbing her temples with two fingers on each side of her head.

"You could go to any physical therapist in the city. Why come here?" Karmyn finally lifted her head and felt an immediate kick in the stomach. Vincent was so attractive. His perfectly trimmed beard made him look even more refined. She had to stop looking at him, so she focused on some documents on her desk.

"When you want the best, you go to the best."

"Maybe another time I would have believed that." When he made no effort to leave, Karmyn gave up. "If you insist, the scheduling desk is out front. You don't need me to help you. What do you really want?"

"I want a second chance."

Karmyn looked directly into his eyes for the first time since he entered her office, and she burst into a fit of laughter. He could have said anything else, and she may have believed him, but wanting a second chance with her was outright hysterical.

"Am I being Punk'd or something? Is this a joke? I would never take you back. So, you can leave now." Karmyn used her hand to shoo him away from her desk. When he didn't take the hint, she stood and stared him straight in the eyes.

"Vincent, you are my past, and nothing good comes from going backward."

"I messed up okay. I admit, I was a dog. I let my ego get to me. But you were the best thing that ever happened to me. We were good together once. You can't deny that. All I want is a chance to show you I have changed. I'm not the same man I was when we divorced. That man was arrogant and selfish. I'm different."

He walked around her desk and held her gaze. She wouldn't back down. She wouldn't show him any emotion. He stood in front of her and used his thumb to tilt her face toward him. "Just give me a chance."

*****

Nick overheard the exchange between Vincent and Karmyn. He couldn't believe that Vincent was serious about reconciling with his ex-wife. Well, actually, he could understand. Nick was also interested in Karmyn, and he wasn't going to let her make the same mistake again. Nick quickly walked away from her office, not wanting to run into Vincent when he left.

Nick had a nagging feeling that something wasn't right. Why would Vincent show up now? He hadn't kept up with his former client's career, but his sudden return needed to be investigated. Nick first needed to get some answers and headed to the barbershop where he knew he would find them.

Sharper Image was unusually crowded for a Monday afternoon. They were one of the few barbershops that opened seven days a week. Nick took notice that Simon's car was missing, but that didn't matter. He needed advice from the patrons. They had better information about local celebrities than TMZ.

Nick walked through the door into a room of laughing and yelling. Several of the barbers and customers were engaged in a spirited conversation of frivolity.

"Here comes the attorney. Let's ask him," Tyrel yelled to the crowd.

"Ask me what?" Nick asked while taking a seat in Simon's empty barber chair.

"If I say, meet me at the club next Friday, are you going this Friday coming up or next week on Friday?" Marquez asked. Marquez was a self-proclaimed barbershop manager when Simon was away. He was the oldest barber in the barbershop and had been with Simon since he opened his first place.

Nick contemplated the question then laughed. This was just like the barbershop to have a debate over nonsense.

"If you tell me today, on Monday, you want me to meet you at the club next Friday, I would assume you meant next week on Friday," Nick answered.

The barbershop went up in a roar, customers were laughing, but Raheem was not. He tried to control his features. Raheem was the newest barber and often showed his anger management issues when things didn't go his way. Simon gave the young man a chance to turn his life around after being released from juvenile detention a few years ago. Simon footed the bill to barber college and kept him close by after he graduated. Being surrounded by men from all walks of life was supposed to be a positive influence on Raheem. The jury was still out.

"Man, come on. Next Friday means the very next Friday, which would be this week," Raheem said, trying to get someone to agree with him.

"Then why not just say meet me at the club this Friday? Or better yet, just say Friday," Nick said.

"That's what we've been trying to tell young school over there," Marquez laughed.

The friendly rivalry between the two barbers was entertaining at best. Raheem had started calling Marquez "Old School" because of the 20-year age difference and his philosophical world views. In response, Marquez kept calling him "Young School."

Once the laughter subsided, Nick jumped in with his own question. "I need some information on Vincent Gallagher."

The shop was quiet for a few minutes as people thought to themselves. Nick looked around to see if anyone knew anything. He almost felt like it was some type of well-kept secret that Nick didn't know about.

"I saw him at the strip club a few months ago. Throwing money in the air in the VIP section," A young man said, sitting against the wall, waiting for Tyrel. Tyrel was another young barber in the shop.

"Yeah, my baby mama said her sister's cousin's, next-door neighbor was dating him. I don't know if I believe anything my baby mama's sister's cousin says," the client getting a line-up from Raheem added.

"Last week, he was down at the Riverwalk with two honeys that looked like twins. That boy has been wilding out since he got divorced." Many of the guys in the barbershop agreed with him.

"Heck, he was wilding out before he got divorced. Stupid. Have you seen his ex-wife? Just as beautiful as her sister, Karleigh," Marquez told Nick.

Nick wouldn't deny that Karmyn and her sisters were beautiful. But, Karmyn had a *je ne sais quoi* that other women didn't have. Sure, she was beautiful and successful, but there was so much more to her.

The barbershop only confirmed Nick's suspicion that Vincent hadn't left his philandering ways. What Nick didn't know was what Vincent was up to. He would have to do some more digging, maybe even hire an investigator to find more information. When it was all over, Vincent would not win Karmyn back.

The conversation quickly moved to sports leaving Nick with his thoughts.

Chapter 9

Karmyn hadn't seen Nick in a few weeks. She thought she would have run into him at least once since they worked in the same building. She knew for sure he had been in the office yesterday. His car had been in his parking space when she arrived at the gym. But when she left for the day, his car was gone.

She felt like he was avoiding her. Their weekend had been amicable and downright fun most of the time. Nick's brothers were very entertaining, and she loved his parents' enthusiasm for life. They reminded her so much of her own parents. So, what could be his reason for not reaching out to her?

If she were honest with herself, why hadn't she called him since they returned? Nick wasn't solely responsible for reaching out. Karmyn had his number and had attempted to call him several times. Ultimately, not dialing his number. She didn't want to seem eager. Her grandmother would tell her and her sisters if a man was interested, he did the calling. Now, her grandmother's advice seemed outdated, yet, she waited on.

After the week she had, all Karmyn wanted to do was relax at home. She tried to sleep in on her day off but was awakened early in the morning by a sudden fit of coughing. Grabbing the water bottle next to her bed, Karmyn downed its contents but still felt that tickle feeling in the back of her throat. By the time she had taken a shower and dressed, she had begun feeling worse.

Her head had started with a low throb around her temples and eased its way behind her eyes. She went in search of some pain reliever when she began noticing she was experiencing some nasal congestion. Three hours later, Karmyn was convinced she had a summer cold. She didn't have a fever, but her other symptoms indicated a head cold. She felt miserable and weak in a matter of hours.

That afternoon, Karmyn was resting on her sofa with an ice pack to her forehead and eyes. She didn't have the energy to move. The only place she had been was to the bathroom, and that took a great effort. Now, someone was at her door, and she could barely lift her phone to check the doorbell camera.

Of course, it was Nick on the other side. He hadn't called her all week, and now he was at her house. Instead of speaking to him through the speaker, she just remotely unlocked her door to allow him inside. She didn't have the strength to battle with him.

"Karmyn?" he yelled from the foyer.

"I'm in the living room," she responded. It sounded like a yell, but probably was just above a whisper. When he entered the room, she began violently coughing again.

"Don't get too close. I may be very contagious." She grabbed the roll of toilet paper that was in her lap, balled up a handful, and tried to empty all of the mucus from her nose.

"You should have warned me before I came inside. I fear I am now infected," Nick joked.

Karmyn wanted to laugh but couldn't. The pain was intensifying through her head. When she opened her eyes, she saw Nick had removed his suit jacket and rolled up his sleeves.

"What are you doing?" Karmyn asked barely above a whisper. Her voice was scratchy and slowly going away.

"I am going to take care of you. Do you have a thermometer?"

Karmyn weakly pointed to the mess beside her on the floor. She had a thermometer, rolls of toilet paper, two empty bottles of water, a bag of throat lozenges, and half a bottle of cold medicine. She was embarrassed that Nick found her in this condition. She was fully dressed but too weak to move.

For the next hour, Nick busied himself, making her a pot of chicken noodle soup. He had her take some decongestant medicine and eat her soup. He also made her some herbal tea with lemon and honey. Karmyn was glad she had everything he needed in her kitchen. She usually kept a well-stocked kitchen. Her healthy lifestyle also included healthy food choices.

After Nick wrapped her in her favorite blanket, he joined her for a movie. He didn't get too close, but stayed and that was what mattered the most to her. He didn't have to do anything else, just being around made her feel better. Even after she told him she could be contagious, he just stepped in and stepped up. She found that endearing—gold star for Nick.

Karmyn later awakened to the soft snoring of Nick stretched out on her floor. The last thing she remembered was watching some movie about aliens before she drifted off to sleep. But that was only after Nick rechecked her temperature and made sure she had plenty of fluids in her system. He even made her a salad for dinner and Jell-O for dessert.

At no time in her entire relationship with Vincent had he done anything so nice and kind for her. His idea of taking care of her when she was sick was to call his mother or hire a nurse.

She felt much better than she had earlier and didn't want to wake him, so she eased from the sofa and placed her blanket over him. He looked so adorable sleeping on her floor. Karmyn stared at him and imagined what it would be like to be in a relationship with Nick. That life was probably filled with parties and events where he needed to schmooze with his clients. She had enough of that life but was suddenly thinking it may be different with Nick. She made sure her doors were locked before heading to her bedroom to sleep.

The following day, Karmyn awakened to the smell of fresh coffee and what she thought was food being cooked. She grabbed her robe from the back of her door and padded her way into the kitchen. Her eyes bulged out at the sight before her. Nick had made breakfast and was now cleaning the kitchen.

"What is going on?" Karmyn looked over the dishes he had prepared. It was more like a buffet for a king instead of just the two of them. He had scrambled eggs, turkey bacon, veggie omelets, French toast, cinnamon rolls, coffee, and juice.

"Good Morning, Sleeping Beauty. I made breakfast. I was just about to wake you after I finished cleaning up in here. Please, have a seat." He pulled her chair out at the breakfast bar. He had place settings out and everything in serving dishes. These were dishes she had received as wedding gifts and never had a chance to use.

"This is such a surprise. I thought you would be gone."

"Nonsense. Now sit and eat," he gave her his signature smile. "How do you like your coffee? "he asked while turning his back to her. Karmyn watched as he poured them both cups of coffee.

"I like my coffee with a lot of sugar." She laughed at his unbelieving expression. "I know I am a fitness junkie, but coffee and sugar are just a few of my many cheats."

"Am I to understand that the health guru loves sugar?" Nick laughed.

"I work out so much because sweets are my weakness." Karmyn lowered her head and said her grace before digging into the dishes.

Nick had made himself a plate of food and sat next to her at the breakfast bar. Together, they ate in silence.

"This is amazing. Who taught you how to cook?" Karmyn asked after she had cleaned her plate and was reaching for second helpings.

"You have met my mother, right? She made sure her boys could survive without the need of anyone else. She taught us all to cook, clean, and sew."

Karmyn was shocked that his mother would teach them so much. Dottie seemed no-nonsense, but anyone could see she spoiled her boys. The weekend she was with the Butlers, Dottie cooked every day. Even on the days she hired catering, she still made several other dishes.

Karmyn bit into a cinnamon roll and sighed at the taste of the sweetness, then realized she didn't have cinnamon rolls in her kitchen. "Where did this come from?" she asked.

"I placed a grocery order when I woke up this morning. I didn't want to disturb you."

Karmyn had a fleeting thought of how she would have enjoyed being interrupted by Nick in the morning. But she shook her head, clearing her mind and took another bite of the cinnamon roll. This entire scenario was a bit too comfortable, and Karmyn felt as if she needed a moment to gather herself.

There was a comfortable, companionable silence between them as they continued eating. She wanted to find something wrong with Nick so she could kick him out. She needed some space and time to figure out her thoughts. But he was the epitome of a gentleman. Her brain was still spinning from his thoughtfulness and caring efforts. Karmyn knew she was stuck at the moment.

Nick broke into her thoughts and asked, "You seem to be feeling much better now. Did you have plans for today?"

*****

Nick certainly hoped she wasn't planning to do anything. He wanted to spend more time with her. Their weekend in Savannah seemed so long ago, but they barely had time to spend alone with each other.

"I am planning to go to church. Then dinner at my parent's house. It's a tradition of sorts." Karmyn said, staring into her empty coffee cup.

"Oh, church," Nick was disappointed.

"That's right, you're spiritual, not religious," she snickered.

He hated that he told her that when they were stuck in the elevator. Nick wasn't opposed to going to church. He just usually had other plans. His mother made sure her boys had a good foundation in faith. Over the years, church didn't feel the same as it had when he was growing up. Now the leaders in the churches were packed with flashy titles, cars, and jewelry. Pastors now had to have security details everywhere they went.

"You don't have to make it sound like that. I go to church sometimes. We went just last weekend with my parents."

"You were forced into that, and you spent most of the time in the bathroom. At least that's where you said you went." She smiled when saying that because she knew he and his brothers had gone outside. She commented that no bathroom break was that long.

Nick didn't know what to say now. She was showing him exactly who she was, a God-fearing woman. It was branded in the name of her gym, she wore her belief like a flashing neon sign, and her actions from work to play were indicative of her faith.

He decided to do something he had never done before. Something that his brothers would say was out of character for him. Before he could ask the question, there was a knock on her door. They seemed confused at the intrusion.

She didn't seem to be expecting anyone. It was 9:00 am on a Sunday. Karmyn shrugged her shoulders at Nick's questioning look and allowed him to answer the door.

The last person in the world Nick expected to see was standing at her door. Vincent was wearing dark shades and a slightly wrinkled suit that looked like he may have slept in it all night. He was sluggish, and his movements were slow. When he finally raised his head and noticed Nick, he tried to straighten up.

"What are you doing here?" he asked.

"I could ask you the same thing." Both men stared at the other, sizing each other up. But Nick had the upper hand. He was in the house, and Vincent was outside.

"Nick, who is it?" Karmyn asked from the hallway leading to the door.

"Karmyn, baby!" Vincent yelled from the door. "Tell your

guard dog to step aside."

"Vincent! What are doing you here?" Nick noticed Karmyn tightened the belt on the robe she had been wearing. She approached the door with raised eyebrows, evident that she was not expecting Vincent.

"That's what I asked him," Nick stood to the side of the door, still blocking Vincent from entering but allowing Karmyn space to stand at his side.

"I thought I'd stop by and take you to church. I figured you had the same routine."

"Yeah, well, Nick is taking me."

Nick was startled when she made that announcement, "I am? I mean, yes, I am."

"When did this start? After the divorce or before it?" Vincent tossed out the accusation. If Nick weren't trying to impress Karmyn, he would have knocked Vincent flat on his back by now. The man dared to show up to her house, drunk, and ask to take her to church.

"That is none of your business."

"You are my wife. It is my business."

"Ex-wife…as in, not married anymore. You can leave."

"Karmyn, we need to talk, alone. Believe me. I have changed."

"I can't tell." She gave him a head-to-toe look and smirked. "Have a blessed day." Karmyn walked away, leaving the men standing off at the door.

"You heard the lady. Vincent, you look like you slept in those clothes, and you haven't taken the shades off. I would bet your eyes are probably red from drinking. Just go home, man."

"You don't know anything about me. And me and Karmyn, we have history. I'm her first love." Vincent probably hadn't noticed that he slurred quite a few words. "I'll leave this time, but I'll be back. Count on that."

Nick closed the door behind Vincent. He stood in the vestibule for a few minutes before heading back toward the kitchen. He needed to unpack the scenario that had just unfolded before him. Karmyn didn't seem vengeful. She appeared calm when she told him to have a blessed day. Nick had expected her to be angry and maybe blow up, but she kept her cool.

He slowly walked back into the kitchen, but Karmyn was gone. She must have gone to her bedroom. He started for the stairs when Karmyn appeared from a door just behind the staircase.

"I know I kind of put you on the spot, telling him you are taking me to church. You don't have to."

"I don't mind."

"Well, if you want to go to church, meet me there at 11:00 am. I can drive myself, but you need to go home and change clothes. You can't wear that." She laughed and walked away.

Nick raced home, quickly showered, and dressed. He was thankful that her church was on his side of town. The parking lot was getting full when he arrived, and he was able to find a parking space near the back of the church.

Nick spotted Simon and Karleigh when they arrived. He joined them by the entrance to the church.

"Hey Nick, what are you doing here?" Simon asked.

"I thought it was time for me to grow closer to Christ."

"Pay up." Karleigh put her hand out and waited for Simon to place a $20 bill in her palm.

"What is that all about?"

"Karleigh bet me you would lie about coming to church this morning. Thanks for making me look bad," Simon smiled.

"Karmyn called me right after you left this morning and told me everything. Thank you for being there for my sister. She sometimes thinks she is a superwoman and doesn't know how to ask for help. Come to think of it, all of my sisters are like that."

"A trait you all seem to share." Simon faked hurt when Karleigh threw a soft punch into his arm.

"Here comes Karmyn now."

Karmyn was dressed in a plum-colored dress that reached just below the knee. The black heels she wore made her calf muscles pop out. It was very apparent Karmyn was physically fit. She pulled her hair back into a tight ponytail and wore very little make-up. Nick admired how beautiful she was without even trying.

Karmyn greeted her sister and brother-in-law before turning to Nick. "Glad you could make it. I didn't think you would show up."

"Turn down an invitation from you? Not in this lifetime."

The two couples sat together in the same pew as the other members of the Hammond Family. It was an unspoken rule that the third pew on the left side of the sanctuary belonged to their family. Karmyn's grandmother made a sizable donation to the church to have her family name on that specific pew. No member dared to sit there. An occasional visitor was allowed.

Grandma Hammond sat next to Dr. Grant Hawkins, who was now Poe's fiancé. Nick had yet to meet the family matriarch. She was at Karleigh's wedding but not at the reception. She claimed the wedding reception would be too much excitement for an old lady.

Praise and worship began with Poe leading the praise team. Their youngest sister, Kyna, was notably absent from the group.

"Where is your younger sister?" Nick whispered to Karmyn.

"She is probably working on the women's day event. She is in the church somewhere."

After several selections from the praise team, the pastor came to the pulpit, loudly cleared his throat, and waited for the church to quiet down.

"Church, please stand to your feet for the reading of the word. Open your bible and turn to Jeremiah 29:11. Let us read, *'For I know the plans I have for you,' declares the LORD, 'plans to prosper you and not to harm you, plans to give you hope and a future.'"*

Today's sermon was about Hope.

Vincent watched Karmyn and Nick from the last pew in the church. His jealousy and anger were growing with every breath. Since their divorce, she had remained single, not even going on a single date. Now that he had a plan in place, she was seeing someone, and it had to be his former attorney. The same guy who dropped him as a client for no reason. Well, he would take care of both of them.

Before the collection plate was passed, Vincent slipped out of the sanctuary unseen. He had to find that business card from last week. An idea was formulating in his brain. For this to happen, he would need her help.

*****

After church service was the annual women's day celebration. The program was filled with more singing and performances by special guests and the children of the church. It was a tradition that the men of the church served the women lunch in the fellowship hall. The sisters were sitting at a table with their significant others. Kyna's husband, Morgan, was out of the country on business.

The seven had finished their desserts when the conversation came around to how you know that God loves you. Unlike the men in their lives, the sisters were raised in the church. Being raised in the church by a praying grandmother and Christian parents, there were a few things you had to remember. Their grandmother had taught them to memorize the meaning of Psalms 23.

"I'll start," Karleigh volunteered. "Look at Psalms 23 verse 1. *The Lord is my shepherd*. That's a relationship. Like Kevin is my father, Kyra is my mother, and Simon is my husband. They are all relationships. God *wants* to have a relationship with you," Karleigh explained.

"*I shall not want* is the supply that He gives to all of us. When we trust in Him, we want for nothing. God provides all of our needs," Poe added.

"*He makes me to lie down in green pastures, He leads me beside the still waters*; that is the rest we all need and the refreshment we are promised," Karmyn said.

"*He restores my soul* is God's healing. *He leads me in the paths of righteousness for His name's sake*, that is God's guidance and purpose over our lives." Kyna said. "These first three verses tell us we have everything we need; our rest, our refreshment, our healed souls, and a path to follow."

By this time, the men were all ears and a few others who overheard the conversation were also intrigued.

"Verse 4 is my favorite. *Yea, though I walk through the valley of the shadow of death, I will fear no evil*. That is the test and the protection that God offers us. *For thou art with me*, is God's faithfulness to us. *Thy rod and staff comfort me*. That is discipline. This verse tells me that even on my darkest days, He is still with me, and I have nothing to fear," Poe said.

"Verse 5 says *Thou prepares a table before me in the presence of my enemies*. Now that's hope. The future that I am preparing for," Karmyn said. "Faith is in the present, but to dream big and know that God will see you through, that's having hope for the future."

"*Thou anoints my head with oil* is the consecration from God. *My cup runs over* is the abundance He promises. When we seek God and believe in His promises to us, our cup will spill with the gifts He has for us," Karleigh said.

"Verse 6 says, *Surely goodness and mercy shall follow me all the days of my life*," Kyna continued.

Together the sisters said, "Now that's a blessing." They laughed at their inside joke.

"*And I will dwell in the house of the Lord forever*. That is God's security, and it is forever an eternity," Karmyn ended. "That is how we were taught God's love for us."

"Face it guys, God loves you," Kyna said. "What is most valuable is not what we have in our lives, but *who* we have in our lives.

A chorus of Amens rang out around the room. The sisters hadn't realized they had an audience and looked around to see many of the congregation standing around.

Nick felt good after church, something akin to a refreshing of his spirit. He headed home thinking about Karmyn, her sisters, and what he learned about faith and hope. Especially what he learned about Psalm 23. Nick had never heard it broken down in that way. The last time he read that passage, it was a memory verse at vacation bible school. No one had ever truly explained it to him.

Now he understood the Hammond sisters much better. They lived their faith out loud. Anyone who took time to get to know the sisters would see they all had a firm foundation built on faith. Nick decided that he wanted to develop a stronger relationship with God. Karmyn had been right that day in the elevator. His being spiritual was a cop-out for not going to church and learning more.

Chapter 10

It had been three months since Nick joined Karmyn at church that first time. Since then, they had gone out a few times. He was becoming a regular at her church on Sunday mornings. Working in the same building also made it convenient for them to have lunch and an occasional dinner.

Neither of them had seen nor heard from Vincent after his unexpected visit to her house. He had not shown up for his first physical therapy appointment after his supposed surgery. Karmyn began wondering if that was just some type of ploy to get to her. Maybe he decided that using a different physical therapy office would be better. Either way, she was in a happy place.

What Vincent did was no longer a matter of Karmyn's. She need not spend another thought on him. She had a thriving business and a man in her life that made her happy. Karmyn smiled at the idea that she and Nick could now be considered friends. Although they had not defined what their relationship was, she was still enjoying life. And in a thousand years, she never would have thought it would be with Nicolas Butler.

Karmyn was getting dressed for dinner with Nick and one of his colleagues. The dinner was important because Nick was deciding whether to bring this attorney on as a partner. She was excited when Nick told her he had made reservations at the Sphere, an elegant, upscale restaurant on the top floor of the tallest building downtown. You could see the entire city from the restaurant.

She decided on a basic black sheath dress and accessorized it with a chunky jeweled necklace and matching bracelet. She was looking for her shoes when the doorbell rang. Looking at the clock, she thought Nick was right on time.

Her mood went from joyous to irritated when she opened the door to find Vincent. He was like a stray cat that kept coming back hoping for food.

"What do you want?" Karmyn asked, not moving from the doorway.

"Can I come in?"

"No."

"You look good. Where are you going?"

Vincent was dressed in a sports running suit and was wearing sunglasses, even though the sun had set. He wasn't his usual suave self. The man in front of her appeared almost desperate. He even looked thinner than he had the last time she saw him.

"That's none of your business. Can you please leave me alone?"

"Karmyn, I'm trying to apologize to you. I love you."

"Sure, you do. Goodbye." Karmyn tried to close the door, but Vincent used his arm to keep the door open. Coming closer to Karmyn, she could smell alcohol seemingly permeating from every pore in his body. A distillery probably smelled better.

"Hear me out. I made a lot of mistakes when we were married. Please give me a chance to show you I have changed," Vincent said, raising his voice.

Neither of them heard Nick approaching.

"Karmyn, are you okay?" Nick brushed past Vincent, staring him up and down.

"I'm fine, thank you. I'm almost ready to leave," she left Nick at the door with Vincent. She needed her shoes and to retrieve her handbag.

"So, you're dating my wife? All of the women in the world, you couldn't find your own?"

"Vincent, she is not your wife any longer."

"It's like that?" He stepped closer to Nick, and Nick wasn't about to back down. The two men stood toe to toe, equal in height, and stared at each other as the boxers do before a heavyweight championship fight. Except in this case, if one of them threw a punch, there would be no referee to break it up.

Karmyn returned to the stand-off between the two men. She pushed her way between them, hoping to end whatever macho ego trip they seemed to be riding. Karmyn was not about to become another story on the nightly news. She could see the headlines now...a Former NFL player caught fighting with his former attorney over his ex-wife. The headlines are not where Karmyn wanted to be for any reason, except maybe at the success of her businesses. When they separated, she pushed them both outside and locked her front door. She had to practically drag Nick to his car.

"Was all of that necessary?" she asked once they were on the road.

"Why was he at your house?" Nick asked through clenched teeth but seemingly trying to stay calm.

"First of all, I don't like the tone you have. Second, I don't know why he was at my house. He was uninvited, just like last time. He has been drinking and still asking that I take him back."

Karmyn was replaying the interaction over in her mind. Vincent seemed always to pick times when Nick was around. Then Nick becoming the jealous boyfriend was a bit too much. She saw a side of Nick that she didn't know. Now, with Vincent constantly showing up, Karmyn wondered if Nick was having a problem dealing with it all.

The remainder of the ride to the restaurant was completed in silence. Karmyn was uneasy with the way things unfolded, yet, again at her doorstep. She was also a little unnerved by Nick's reaction and subsequent accusation. Did he think she had invited Vincent to her home when he was on his way?

So many thoughts were swirling in her mind. The one that kept returning was maybe they were moving too fast, and maybe Nick was not the man for her. He had turned on the smooth jazz station to fill the silence. The music was soothing to her frayed nerves and erratic thoughts.

By the time they arrived at the restaurant, both of their tempers had eased. Nick apologized for his behavior and complimented her attire. Karmyn accepted his apology but was still uneasy about something. Despite it all, they were able to enjoy a wonderful evening. That was until Vincent showed up again around dessert time.

Karmyn could not believe that he had followed them. What did he expect would happen? She could see Nick flexing his fist under the table. He had a fire in his eyes, and this time if Vincent tried something, Nick would surely finish it.

"What's up, Nick? Karmyn? Fancy meeting you two here."

"Vincent, don't do this, not here," Karmyn pleaded with him just above a whisper.

"Why not? You don't want people to know you are dating my lawyer." He was loud enough that the surrounding tables heard his outburst. Vincent grabbed a chair from a nearby table and dragged it across the floor, making a hideous screeching sound. That drew the attention of almost everyone in the restaurant.

"Vincent, have you been drinking?" Nick asked.

"Not enough." Vincent grabbed the half-filled wine glass from in front of Karmyn and downed the contents before taking the glass from in front of Nick and drinking his too. "Let me tell you something. Karmyn is my wife. Mine. You can't have her." Vincent yelled before knocking the chair over and storming away.

Karmyn was humiliated and mortified as the other patrons openly stared at their table. She could hear Nick profusely apologizing to his colleague and her wife, but the sounds were getting muffled. She felt like the room was spinning but in slow motion. She had to get away from the table, away from the judging eyes, and away from Nick.

Without a word, Karmyn stood and walked away toward the ladies' room. Her feet felt heavy and slowed her steps. She felt like a circus attraction as people continued to look and whisper. Finally making it to the ladies' room, Karmyn collapsed on a sofa in the sitting area and allowed her tears to free fall.

Karmyn stayed in the ladies' room until one of the restaurant's servers came in to tell her that Nick was waiting. She didn't know how long she had stayed in there, but she wasn't ready to leave just yet. The embarrassment alone is what kept her unable to face the outside.

There was a soft knock on the door, then Nick's voice. "Karmyn, everyone is gone. Let me take you home."

Karmyn was sitting in her office one afternoon after treating her staff to lunch. Her focus was supposed to be on her financial records, but she kept thinking back to Nick. He was scheduled to be in court all day, and they probably would not see each other. She had not seen him since the night at the restaurant, and that had been three days ago. He had sent her text messages, short and sweet. This had been the longest they had gone without seeing each other since they started dating.

Everything had been going well until Vincent had to show up. Now she wondered where she and Nick stood. The constant worry about the future of their relationship had her mindless. Karmyn was unable to focus on one thing for any length of time. She tossed her pencil across her desk when she heard a knocking at her door.

"Hey, sis!"

"Hey Simon, what are you doing here?"

Simon was always a welcome face. He was the perfect man for her sister and the perfect brother-in-law.

"I was in the building and thought I would check on my sister-in-law."

"Well, I'm glad you did. Come on in and sit down." Simon was a great distraction from everything she was thinking about. Even though Simon and Nick were best friends, seeing her brother-in-law brought a smile to her face.

"I was just looking at some building space for a possible new location and…."

"Stop! What is it with this family? Why does everyone all of a sudden want to move into this building? Karleigh, Nick, then Kyna and Morgan, and now you. Did any of you ever think I want to have space from you people?"

Simon laughed, "When you say '*you people*,' I hope you don't really mean your family. The very people that love and support you."

"Geez, now you want to make me feel bad."

"Seriously, would it be so bad to have your family in the building? You are only here what, three days a week. You have two other locations where you can spend your time. I don't know about Morgan and Kyna, but I am looking to expand, not work here. So, I would not be underfoot," Simon explained.

If she were honest with herself, it wouldn't be so bad having her sisters in the building with her. That would save on having to drive across the city, back and forth, to see one another.

"What about your best friend? Tell the truth, why did Nick move his office?"

"A little bit had to do with you, but mostly, the office he was in was going up on the rent, and he found a better deal here."

They talked for a few more minutes before Simon had to leave for another appointment. "Oh, by the way, I didn't know you and Vincent were back on speaking terms."

Karmyn jerked her head up to see if Simon was joking.

"What made you think that?"

"Because he was in the gym working out when I came in."

Karmyn felt her temper rising. She had started her morning off on a happy note, and now she felt her world turning upside down. Trying to school her facial feature to not indicate her anger, she walked Simon to the front door and then proceeded to the therapy side of the gym, where she found Vincent flirting with one of the trainers.

"What are you doing here?"

"I told you, I need to rehab. You have the best place for that."

"Your surgery was over three months ago. Why are you here now? You must have been rehabbing somewhere." Karmyn was failing at keeping her cool, visibly becoming frustrated.

Vincent gave her a smirk that irritated Karmyn almost to the point of fury. She clenched and unclenched her fist, not sure if she would knock that smirk off his face.

Through clenched teeth, Karmyn said, "Vincent, the moment you being here interferes with my business, I will ban you from the facility. Do I make myself clear?"

"Perfectly," Vincent winked at her.

Karmyn wanted to scream, but doing so would cause a greater scene than they had now. She was about to walk away when Vincent grabbed her arm and pulled her back against his chest.

*****

That was all Nick needed to see. Vincent appeared to be forcefully stopping her movement. He would not allow Vincent or anyone to put their hands on his woman. Nick was thankful court ended early and that Simon had called him to let him know Vincent was in the gym. He stopped what he was doing and made his way to the first floor. Nick rushed in and immediately snatched Karmyn from Vincent's embrace.

"Hey man, what do you think you're doing?" Nick shouted.

"I was talking to my wife, if you don't mind," Vincent responded with a smug smile on his face.

"Yeah, well, did your ex-wife want to talk to you?"

"Nick, please stay out of this," Karmyn pleaded.

Nick had an unkind look in his eyes as he took a step backward, pushing Karmyn behind him. He tried to keep his cool, but Nick was tired of this game that Vincent was playing. He had yet to figure out what Vincent wanted from Karmyn. Barbershop rumors were still flying around about his sleeping around.

"Vincent, it's apparent that Karmyn does not want you here. Why do you insist on harassing her?"

"Hey Karmyn, tell your guard dog to stand down. I'm only here getting rehab for my knee."

"Nick, I asked you to stay out of this. Meet me in my office now." Karmyn stomped toward her office.

She was pacing behind her desk, massaging her temples with her forefingers, when he entered. Nick could tell that he was about to be read the riot act. He allowed his jealousy and overprotectiveness to jump in where it wasn't needed.

"Nick, I do not need your help. I am not a damsel in distress. You do not have to defend me."

"I don't like the way he comes down here, and he inserts himself into your life."

"Well, I don't like that you come down here and throw accusations at my client."

"Oh! So now he is a client?"

"I have an understanding with Vincent. As long as he stays on the rehab side and does not cause issues, he is a paying client. And I cannot afford to lose any paying clients."

Nick just stared at her. She wasn't this naïve to believe anything that Vincent was saying. Vincent had shown up to her home twice, drunk out of his mind, professing his love for her. He wouldn't believe that she would be gullible enough to let him back into her life. He watched her pacing back and forth, trying to think of something to say. He opened his mouth to ask her why, but she cut him off.

"And this whole jealous routine, it needs to stop. As a matter of fact, *we* need to stop. *We* are not a couple. *We* were just having some fun, and now it ends."

"Karmyn, what are you saying?" Nick couldn't believe that she was calling their relationship just something fun to do. He thought they had grown closer and was working toward developing a long-term connection.

"I'm saying we will no longer do lunch or dinner anymore. It was fun, but this has to stop."

He stood there in disbelief, shaking his head. This couldn't be happening. For the first time, he thought he had found a woman he would want to spend his life with. Karmyn was everything he didn't know he wanted, and she was throwing it all away.

She stood there with her arms folded over her chest and staring at him, waiting for Nick to say something. When, after several minutes, he didn't say anything, she brushed past him and opened her office door wide.

"Nick, I have work to do. If you don't mind."

Now Nick was fuming. He had never been dumped or asked to leave by a woman. He was Nicolas Butler, attorney to the stars. She would not stomp on his pride. Nick held his head high and walked closer to Karmyn than the door. When she looked down at her feet, Nick knew she still had feelings in there somewhere. That gave him hope.

He brushed a finger down the side of her cheek and said, "I will see you again. Very soon. This isn't over."

Nick was furious. As he walked out of her office and back into the gym, he saw Vincent smiling at him. There was no way Nick would allow Vincent to carry out whatever game he was playing. He needed some advice and reinforcement of the best kind. And Nick knew precisely who to talk to and where to go.

Chapter 11

Karmyn called her sisters as soon as she got home. She needed them right now. They were more experienced in the dating world and would know what to do in her situation. Karleigh was married and had other relationships before meeting Simon. Poe was usually a voice of reason, that was until she met Grant. Now she is all lovey-dovey and flowers and hearts. Kyna was the no-nonsense sister and recently married after falling in love at first sight and marrying Morgan after only knowing him for a week. Maybe Kyna wasn't the best person to seek advice.

Since Vincent was her first boyfriend and her first love, Karmyn had no idea what she was doing in the dating world. Fifteen minutes after the emergency sisters' bat-signal text was sent, Poe and Kyna rang her doorbell. Ten minutes later, Karleigh breezed through the door with four bottles of wine and two large pizzas.

Karmyn told her sisters everything about her relationship with Nick from beginning to end, leaving nothing out.

"So, tell me this, sister," Kyna started. "Were you enjoying yourself spending time with Nick?"

"Yes, I was having fun with Nick," Karmyn answered quickly and honestly. The two of them having fun was never in question.

"So, his jealousy is what upset you? Morgan has a jealous

streak that often needs to be doused with my special brand of love. But then again, I get a little jealous, too," Kyna admitted.

"You *should* get jealous when women get too close to Morgan. He is fine and rich," Poe added.

Karleigh opened a bottle of wine and poured everyone a glass. "Poe, seriously, Grant ain't exactly chopped liver in the looks or the banking department either."

"All I'm saying is if he is the jealous type, then I don't want anything to do with him. He showed his true colors at the gym today." Karmyn had never had to deal with jealousy from Vincent. It was a new emotion for her. The thought of a man getting angry or upset about her felt controlling, and she didn't like it.

The sisters became silent, each taking a sip of their wine and in their own thoughts. This was how the evening would go. They would talk, then think, then talk some more. Each sister had a different perspective and experience when it came to dating. Karmyn wanted to hear it all.

"So, what do I do?" Karmyn asked. "Karleigh, you're the oldest and most experienced. Help me."

"Dang, sister. Make me sound like a harlot, why don't you?" Karleigh laughed to lighten the mood.

"I didn't mean it like that."

"My suggestion is to talk with Nick. Tell him how you feel. And tell him you need to take things slow. But when it comes to Vincent to let you handle things."

"Honestly, I think that may be a good idea. Especially if you still want to date him," Poe added.

"No matter what you decide, your sisters are here for you. And if we need to break his kneecaps, I know people." Kyna winked at her sisters because that was Karmyn's favorite line to say when her sisters would bring new guys around.

All four bottles of wine were empty, and the sisters were laid out across the rug in Karmyn's living room, finishing off the last of the pizza. Kyna and Poe decided to stay the night, not sure they would be able to drive home. No one noticed that Karleigh had barely sipped one glass of wine. Since she was sober, she decided to sneak out after the sisters were fast asleep.

Karleigh knew Simon was at the barbershop and, after a few text messages, found out that Nick was there too. She had a few things to tell him.

*****

"Simon, what am I doing?" Nick asked, taking a swig from his beer bottle. He was reclining in a barber chair, watching Simon clean up the barbershop.

"I need more information before I can help with that question." Simon inquired.

"With Karmyn. Why am I pushing for this relationship with her?"

"Ahh, I see. The forever bachelor is getting a taste of love."

"Love? Whoa, Brother, slow down. No one said anything about love. Infatuation maybe, lust probably, but no love." Nick wasn't ready to admit to his friend that he had been having thoughts about forever with Karmyn. But he wasn't sure if that would be considered love. Saying it out loud would make it real, and Nick wasn't sure he was ready for that.

Simon laughed and continued sweeping the floor. The silence was broken when Karleigh entered the shop. She immediately went to Simon and kissed him, then stood by her husband and glared at Nick.

"What did I do?" Nick asked.

"Seriously, Nick? Why is Karmyn crying her eyes out because of you?"

"I didn't do anything. Vincent started it."

"You sound like a child. Grow up. Karmyn has been through

enough heartache."

"She dumped me." Nick hated how he seemed to be the bad guy in all of this. But seeing Vincent with his hands on Karmyn caused something inside of him to explode. She was his woman, and he wouldn't allow any man or woman to bring her harm. Even as he said those words in his head, he sounded too possessive. Maybe he took the wrong approach, but he won't apologize for his intent.

"You and your crazy, jealousy tendencies, trying to be a hero. But Karmyn can take care of herself. She doesn't need a hero. She needs a friend." Karleigh softened her blow toward him. She was truly a loving big sister.

Nick thought about Karleigh's words. Was he a friend for Karmyn or a man on a mission? He thought about the time they spent together. There were getting to know each other, and that's what friends do. But maybe he wasn't being a true friend where she was concerned. After leaving the barbershop, he drove around the city and thought about what it meant to be a friend. A friend is letting the other person be themselves, listening to them without judgment. Being a friend meant being there when they needed you and not taking control of the situation. That is where Nick failed.

Nick realized he didn't need to solve Karmyn's problem with Vincent. She wasn't naïve at all. She was smart and could probably see right through Vincent's lies. He laughed at himself for being a fool in front of her. A friend would have let her handle things and stood by to be supportive.

The following day, Nick sent Karmyn a text message asking to meet him for lunch to talk. When she didn't respond, he hoped she would still show up anyhow. After all, the pastor at her church said you had to have faith and hope. They worked hand-in-hand. Well, he had faith she got the message, and he hoped she would show up.

Nick arrived early so not to miss Karmyn if she came. He grabbed a booth in the back of the restaurant so they could have a little privacy. An apology seemed too little. He wanted her to understand that their friendship meant a lot to him.

"Fancy seeing you here."

"Gianna, what are you doing in town?" This was the last person Nick wanted to see, especially when he wasn't sure of where he stood with Karmyn.

"Just wanted to do some sightseeing. I got a taste for Italian and came in. Didn't expect to see you here." Gianna eased into the booth across from Nick.

"Please don't sit. I am expecting someone."

"Is it a woman? Nick, you are such a playboy. Weren't you just in Savannah with a woman?"

Nick was sure Gianna was playing some kind of game. She was a master at manipulation and drama. The only problem was what game was she playing now? Nick stood up, hoping to give Gianna a hint, but she didn't immediately move.

They stared at each other, playing a game of chicken to see who would cave first. This was a game Nick intended to win.

Gianna finally gave up and stood from her seat. She reached over and placed a kiss on his cheek. "See you later, Nick." Nick closed his eyes and silently counted to five. When he opened them, Karmyn was standing in his face.

"Am I too early? Playing us a little too close, aren't you?"

"What? No, I wasn't here with her." Nick wasn't sure if she was still angry with him. He felt knots in his stomach and tried to look nervous.

"Sure, and she didn't kiss you either," Karmyn stated, pointing to the lipstick on his face.

Nick quickly grabbed his handkerchief from his pocket and wiped the red stain away.

"Please, have a seat. Thank you for coming. I didn't think you would," he signaled for the server.

"I started not to. Nick, this can't," she was interrupted by the server who came to take their order.

"I'm not staying long. A glass of water is fine."

Nick placed his order and waited for the server to walk away. "Karmyn, please let me say this." When she didn't say anything, he continued. "I was wrong. I got a little upset seeing Vincent manhandle you like that. I know you can take care of yourself, and it was presumptuous of me to jump in as I did. I just want us to be friends, hang out like we were doing. It was fun. Tell me you weren't having fun, and I will stop right now."

Karmyn eyed him suspiciously, and Nick could feel her sizing him up. He patiently waited for her to respond.

Taking a deep breath and sighing before giving her a response. "Let me think about it."

"It's not a no, so I will take whatever you give." Nick flashed his signature smile.

"Not like you had a choice. But I do need to leave. I'll call you later." She stood and left Nick sitting there with a huge grin on his face.

*****

Karmyn wasn't sure about Nick and his intentions, but she had to give him a chance. He deserved it, unlike Vincent. This time around with Nick, she did not plan to spend as much time with him. She needed to slow things down. Her sisters kept saying they were dating, and she knew they were right. But Karmyn wasn't sure she was ready for a relationship.

Outside of the restaurant, Karmyn retrieved her cell phone from her purse, intending to call Morgan. He had a guy that did undisclosed work as needed. This mess started with Vincent showing up, and she wanted to know what he was up to and needed to know as soon as possible.

"Excuse me, Karla, right? You were at the Butlers' anniversary party in Savannah."

"My name is Karmyn, and you are Gianna. I didn't know you lived in the area." Karmyn tried to dismiss her and walk away, but

Gianna took a few extra steps and jumped in front of her.

"I don't live here. It's cute, but nothing like the beauty of the south. I guess I will see you around."

Karmyn stopped walking and took the bait. "Why would you think that?"

"Because I am here to take care of some unfinished business. Namely with Nick. We have some unresolved feelings, and I think there is something there. I felt at the party."

"Really? Does he know that?"

"He will. His brothers told me you two weren't dating, so I figured this was the best time to remind him of the happiness we once shared."

Karmyn was sure she got that line from a song. She stood there and let Gianna attempt to boast in her revelation of her feelings for Nick. He was fair game if it were a game. But over the last few weeks of getting to know him, Karmyn learned that Nick didn't like games.

"Good luck," Karmyn told her and continued down the streets. Maybe Morgan's guy could look into Gianna as well.

Chapter 12

Nick was having a good day. He didn't see Karmyn the rest of the week until church on Sunday morning. She had texted or called him every day, but their lunch and dinner dates had halted. He accepted her decision and felt that spending time away from one another helped them grow closer.

He was sitting in his office on a rare Tuesday morning. The office was peaceful, and he didn't have to be in court. There was a new case sitting on his desk that seemed to be straightforward. Nick would give this one to a junior associate.

There was still no word from Mr. Haney's attorney. Nick figured they were preparing to drop the lawsuit. Karmyn's gym had a solid contract that included an arbitration clause. Mr. Haney wouldn't get far with his frivolous lawsuit. Nick had found two other cases Mr. Haney had filed that were later dismissed.

"Mr. Butler, Morgan Hawkins is on Line 2, and there is a Ms. Sinclair here to see you. She doesn't have an appointment, but she insisted you would meet with her," his assistant interrupted his thoughts.

"Thank you, Angela. Have Ms. Sinclair wait for me in conference room B."

"Yes, sir."

Nick grabbed his desk phone and connected to Morgan.

"Good Morning. Thanks for getting back to me."

"No problem. I heard you need some help from my guy?"

Morgan's guy was Carlton, a former military special ops guy. He had a way to find information on just about anyone. His particular skill set was beneficial to Morgan and his line of work. Being a billionaire often attracted people of the worst kind.

"Yes, Vincent Gallagher. He has returned and is trying to get back into Karmyn's good graces. Something is definitely up with this guy. Also, I have a problem with a former girlfriend."

"I heard you were sniffing around my sister-in-law. You know, I take my duties as big brother very seriously, which is why I had my guy start looking into Vincent when he first resurfaced. It seems as though Vincent is having some serious money issues. Bad investments, gambling, and the money he had is paying for child support to three different women. The man is broke, and he sees Karmyn as a source of money. Her gyms are doing good."

"Interesting. I knew it was no coincidence that Vincent just suddenly appeared after these years. Have you told Karmyn yet?"

"No. The full report is not complete. I will have my guy send it to you when it's ready."

"Thanks, Morgan. I appreciate it."

"So, should I start thinking of you as a brother-in-law?"

"I'm leaving that up to God," Nick laughed.

"I'll get my guy on your other issue. Just send me her name."

"Thanks."

Nick sat at his desk for a few minutes after ending his call. He had two younger brothers, a plethora of fraternity brothers but never thought about a brother-in-law relationship. Grant and Morgan seemed to be real stand-up guys. Poe and Kyna could do worse than to marry a doctor and a billionaire.

He smiled at the thought of gaining more brothers and possibly getting married to Karmyn one day. That thought didn't scare him as it once had. He just hoped when the time came, she believed in him enough to say yes.

"Mr. Butler. Ms. Sinclair is still waiting for you in Conference room B."

Nick had almost forgotten about Gianna. He grabbed the file on his desk and his jacket. He was not planning to return to the office after lunch. Angela was returning from the conference room with a frown upon her face.

"She is a trip," Angela tossed as she passed Nick.

Nick knew exactly what she meant. The number one reason he and Gianna didn't work out was her attitude of feeling privileged. She also believed that people who were not of her social standing were beneath her. The straw was when she called Nigel a waste of space and education because he chose to work with the Innocence Project instead of making millions in entertainment law like Nick.

Gianna was standing at the windows overlooking the downtown area. When Nick entered the room, she turned and gave him a displeasing look.

"You need to fire her," Gianna announced.

"And why would I do that?" Nick watched her approach and took a seat at the table.

"She asked me if I would like water, then she brought me this cheap plastic bottle of toxic waste. Tell me you have Perrier in this office."

Nick ignored her and sat across from her at the conference table. "What do you want, Gianna? I know you did not travel this far for vacation."

"Nicky, I missed you. Last weekend, I talked to your mother, and she told me that you weren't serious about anyone. I thought that maybe we could talk."

Nick knew Gianna was lying. There was no way that his mother would tell anyone that he wasn't seeing someone. Especially since Dottie believed he and Karmyn were in a dating relationship.

"Gianna, we said all there was to say years ago. You and I will never be."

"Oh Nicky, that little thing with your brother was taken the wrong way. I just wanted what was best for him."

"It's time for you to leave."

"So, you would rather have that gym rat over me? I'm perfect, I have the right connections, and I look good on your arm. What does she have that I don't?"

"Class. Have a nice trip back to Savannah." Nick opened the door for her to leave.

"This is not over." Gianna stormed from the room, swinging her hair from side to side.

Nick was shocked that she had only gotten worse over the years. Her spoiled, rich-girl attitude would be her downfall. He was sure of it. She would be miserable for the rest of her life. She was the same little girl that he dated years ago. If she didn't get what she wanted, Gianna would pout, stomp and throw a tantrum.

Nick delivered the case file to a junior associate on his way out of the building. Instead of taking the elevator, he decided on the stairs. He stopped in the lobby when he saw Gianna and Vincent talking a little too intimately. How did they know each other, Nick wondered? This had to have something to do with Vincent getting back into Karmyn's life. Instead of going to lunch as planned, Nick headed over to Simon's barbershop.

The barbershop was crowded, but this was normal for Simon. He had a reputation for having the best barbers in the city.

"What brings you by in the middle of the day?" Simon asked.

"I need some advice, and everyone knows the best advice is found in the neighborhood barbershop." Many of the patrons agreed with Nick.

"Well, have a seat, and let us have it."

"I have finally come to terms that Karmyn is my future."

A loud cheer went up among the barbers and a few of the

regular customers. Most of them knew Karmyn because she frequented her sister's salon, which was right next door.

"Brother, I know Karmyn. What makes you want a woman like that? She has a sharp tongue," Marquez asked.

"She is only like that with you because you don't know boundaries. What you call harmless flirting is annoying and boarder line sexist sometimes," Nick defended Karmyn. He realized he did that more often than not. Coming to her defense was the very thing she didn't want, but he couldn't help himself.

"Listen, I know how to handle Karmyn. Sure, she is a strong-minded woman. I wouldn't want her another way. She is caring and faithful and the fiercest of any woman I know. Karmyn has had to be guarded to protect herself from these low-lifes who have tried to take her kindness for weakness. That's because when she loves, she loves hard. I don't let her strength scare me away. It's attractive. Karmyn has endured more pain than you can imagine, yet she still has faith in others and hopes for the future. I admire that about her. I just need to be patient with her. She will let me in once I show her that I too am a strong-willed person who can take control without controlling her and that I am trustworthy and will never disrespect her."

"Sounds like you have this all figured out, so what do you need advice about?" Simon asked.

Nick realized he didn't need their advice. Everything he needed for a relationship with Karmyn, he already had.

"You're right. I don't need anything. Let me get out of here. I need to take care of something."

*****

Karmyn sat in her office reading the report from Morgan's guy about Vincent. She was almost fooled into thinking that maybe her ex-husband had changed. But he had not. He was worse now than ever before. She knew he had money issues, but not to this extent.

That was why she had always kept a separate bank account, secret from what even Vincent knew about while they were married. Ms. Velma warned her he didn't know how to hold on to his money.

He made millions of dollars and would blow thousands on fancy cars, European trips, and his women. But the one thing from the report that she didn't know was he had three children, all the same age. She felt her heart tighten again, and the pain was unreal.

"Knock, knock," Vincent announced himself. "I wanted to see if I could take you lunch."

"With what money," she answered dryly.

She looked up from the report and could only see the confusion on his face. "Vincent, I know. I know everything."

"What are you talking about? I just want to talk with you and get some lunch."

"You've got a little better at lying. I almost believed you. I was close to falling for your lies again. I'm so much smarter now. You can take your crap and go back to Houston. That is where your children live, right. All three of them."

Karmyn flinched at the surprised look Vincent had. She couldn't believe he would try to hurt her again. He was a selfish, self-centered, materialistic boy because you couldn't call him a man. What kind of person would try to use people to their own benefit?

"Who told you that?" Vincent fumbled over his words.

"Doesn't matter. I know. And to think, while you were out populating the earth, I was having a miscarriage." The shock on his face told her she needed to tell him. "When you and your lawyer were plotting against me to take everything I earned and worked for while married to you, I was pregnant. That day in the lawyer's office, I lost our child when we signed the divorce papers. I grieved for the child we had talked about, not knowing you had three other children in Texas."

"I didn't know," Vincent whispered, having the nerve to look contrite.

"It doesn't matter now. What matters is I know what you are about. What you have always been about. You have a gambling problem and three children, but somehow you thought you could get in good with me and try what? Get remarried so you could get my money? Or maybe you thought I would give you a loan or something."

Vincent stood there speechless. For the first time, Karmyn realized what she had always known. He wasn't ever going to be the man she dreamed he would be. Their marriage was never real. Karmyn felt a sense of release for a moment when she realized she was finally over all things Vincent Gallagher.

Suddenly, like a clicking puzzle piece, Karmyn accepted that all she had ever hoped for was happening for her. She was finally emotionally free from Vincent, and her business was thriving beyond measure. And, she had someone special to share her success with. Karmyn may not have hoped for Nick specifically, but God didn't make mistakes.

Vincent was still standing in her office, looking confused. Karmyn had never wanted to destroy his life, but she held the power. Ms. Velma had predicted her son's downfall and had prepared for him to mess up his life.

"Look, Vincent, leave me alone. You've got bigger fish to fry. You seem to always forget your mother's will. I get your entire inheritance if you have children outside of your marriage. If you leave now, I won't call the attorney of her estate." Karmyn smiled while saying, "Have a nice life."

The look on Vincent's face would forever be etched into her memory. Karmyn wanted to laugh out loud. Vincent did forget that she held the ace card and could destroy him. Hopefully, Vincent would not be returning. Karleigh walked into the office soon after Vincent left.

"What's that goofy look on your face for?"

"I have finally rid myself of a situation that lasted too long. Vincent is gone."

"Thank you, Jesus." Karleigh started to mimic church shouting, then Karmyn joined in. Before long, the two of them were seriously shouting their praises to God. After several minutes of just giving God the glory, they quieted down and cried happy tears.

"I feel a tremendous weight off my shoulders. I feel so free," Karmyn whispered.

"I'm happy for you, sister. Now, what about Nick?"

"Nick?" In their impromptu praise break, Karmyn had temporarily forgotten about Nick.

"Yes, the man you have been dating for the past few months."

"I need to talk to him. He has been so patient with me. Sticking with me through my moments of insanity. How could he want to be with me when half the time, I didn't want to be with me?"

"I think you need to tell him sooner than later. He is a good guy. A little flashy for my taste," Karleigh laughed.

The sisters sat around Karmyn's office laughing and joking. Karmyn missed moments like this with her sisters. They had all been so busy living lives lately they had forgotten to make time for one another. Pamper weekend once a month had dwindled to once a quarter. Then, finding a time where everyone was free became an obstacle. Karmyn made it her silent mission to get her sisters back together on a regular basis.

Karleigh was telling a story about one of her clients when Karmyn heard her phone ringing in the distance.

"Sis, let me get this." She walked over to her desk and found her cellphone in her desk drawer. The number did not look familiar, and Karmyn paused before answering. "Hello?"

"Karmyn, I just wanted you to believe in me."

"Vincent? Why are you calling me? I said all I needed to say." Karmyn was exasperated having the same conversation with him. While he talked, she also noticed a hitch in his voice. He didn't sound like himself.

"Well, I didn't say all I needed. If you had just listened to me and not to the world, you would see that despite my flaws, I have changed. But instead, you take up with my attorney. You two were probably in on the whole thing from the beginning."

Vincent was rambling on, and Karmyn didn't know what to do. She motioned for her sister to come near and listen to him talking. Nothing he was saying was making sense. Then he went into a tirade about his mother loving Karmyn more than him. As they listened, allowing him just to keep talking, Karleigh called Simon.

"Vincent, where are you?"

"What does it matter? My life is ruined. You had the power to help me, and you didn't. All I wanted was for you to give me another chance. For all of your Christian talk about forgiveness, you didn't even give me a chance."

Now Karmyn was getting nervous. Vincent was beginning to say things like he didn't see another way out, and things got out of control. He still wasn't making any sense, but Karmyn wanted to keep him on the phone until she could figure out what to do.

Time seemed to tick by slowly, and Karmyn still had no idea where Vincent was. Karleigh motioned for her to keep him talking.

"Vincent, I'm sorry I didn't listen to you, but I'm listening now. Where are you?"

"It doesn't matter."

"Yes, it does. You matter. To your children, to me. You matter."

There was an eerie silence on the line. Karmyn hoped he was still there. She quickly prayed he had not done anything crazy. Then she heard police sirens and released the breath she was holding. The sirens seemed to get louder and louder until she realized the police were outside of her building.

"Vincent! Vincent! Are you there? Vincent!" Karmyn screamed into the phone before hearing the connection end.

One of the gym's trainers came into Karmyn's office. "Karmyn, you need to come see this."

Karmyn and Karleigh followed the instructor into the cardio

area, where clients and staff were gathered around. The televisions were broadcasting the same breaking news.

Chapter 13

Isaiah 40:31 (NIV) but those who hope in the LORD will renew their strength. They will soar on wings like eagles; they will run and not grow weary, they will walk and not be faint.

Karmyn couldn't believe what she was watching. She had an out-of-body experience. Until Karleigh touched her, Karmyn had forgotten she was in her gym, surrounded by people. The scene unfolding was truly unbelievable.

Vincent was on the roof of her building, threatening to jump. There were police present, attempting to talk him down, but he kept screaming for Karmyn. She was mortified. Why was he doing this?

"I never took Vincent for someone who would take his life." Karmyn heard her sister talking, but she sounded far away. Suddenly, the camera switched to a witness in front of the building.

"I just met Vincent today in the gym, and he seemed unstable. Then I heard him say his wife was leaving him. I think he must really love her for him to hurt in this way."

Still in shock, Karmyn heard the words Gianna was saying to

the reporter. She wasn't a client in her gym. The woman didn't even live in the city. Nothing was making much sense. How did Nick's ex-girlfriend play into this drama?

As they watched the scene unfold, the crowd grew larger inside her gym and outside. Poe had arrived with Grant, and Kyna had texted that she was on the way. Karleigh was still talking to Simon on the phone, away from everyone.

Karmyn tried concentrating on the television screen but was startled by yelling coming from the gym's front. Several reporters were attempting to enter her facility. They were yelling and shouting questions across the room. Grant ran over to assist the staff with keeping the reporters back.

The room began spinning for Karmyn, and she felt herself being lifted from the ground and carried back into her office. Like a knight in shining armor, Nick was there, and then he was gone. When she opened her eyes, Karmyn was lying on the sofa in her office, and she could hear whispered voices. Had she passed out? Maybe she had a bad dream, and Vincent wasn't really trying to end his life.

"Welcome back."

Karmyn opened her eyes and found Nick smiling down at her. Karleigh sat on her desk, still talking on the phone. She assumed her sister was talking to Simon or maybe her parents. That meant that the Vincent ordeal was real. Oh no, her parents were probably watching everything. The news that former NFL superstar was attempting suicide was on every network.

"Karmyn, don't sit up. Just rest," Nick instructed her.

"What's going on? How long was I out? Where is Vincent?"

"Too many questions. Let me get you some water first."

Karmyn grabbed his arm, stopping him from walking away. "No! Tell me. What is going on?"

Her heart was racing, anticipating his next words. Did Vincent jump? Was this all her fault for not believing he had changed? So many thoughts ran through her mind that she had to calm herself down to hear what Nick was telling her.

"Karmyn, you passed out for only a few minutes. Vincent is still on the roof, but he isn't going to jump."

"What do you mean? How do you know this?"

"Because it was all a game to get money from you. When you are ready, the police want to talk with you."

Completely perplexed, Karmyn sat in her office, trying to understand. Vincent was playing a game, and how did Gianna fit into all of this? Again, nothing was making sense. Her life since meeting Vincent had been one dramatic event after another. Yet, she had convinced herself she still had a love for Vincent. Even after the humiliation, the infidelity, and the lies, she still hoped that one day Vincent would be the man he promised he would be. Even now, in her heart, she knew who he was but couldn't believe he would stoop this low.

After speaking with the police, Karmyn found that Vincent had a more extensive plan than to just steal money from her. Gianna and Mr. Haney were also in on the scheme. Vincent was in severe debt and owed a few casinos in Vegas money. In one of his drunken states, he divulged that Karmyn had a large sum of money due to the success of her fitness gyms.

Mr. Haney, whose real name was Franklin Duval, a career criminal, had convinced Vincent that he would fake an accident in her gym. Duval had several aliases he used from state to state. Because Vincent knew she didn't like drama, he figured she would allow the insurance company to settle in court. They hadn't counted on Nick representing her. Gianna came into the picture later when she discovered that Karmyn was Vincent's ex-wife. The two had met after Gianna came to town.

Gianna intended to blackmail Karmyn with some altered photos she had taken from the Butlers' anniversary party. The idea was to release them to the press when Vincent got back into her good graces. Vincent would then swoop in like the hero. Gianna had already received an advance for the images from a salacious tabloid and was expected to get more.

Karmyn's head was spinning from all of the information. Once the police left and had taken Vincent, Gianna, and Franklin Duval into custody, Karmyn sat in her office trying to figure out where she went wrong. Her sisters were there with her through every sordid detail. At some point, a police officer even mentioned Vincent may have resulted to abduction. A firearm and zip ties were found in his gym bag.

Grant made sure to close the facility and lock the doors after the police left. Karleigh and Simon were together in one corner, talking with Nick in whispered tones. Poe was sitting on one side of Karmyn and Kyna on the other side, both rubbing her back in a soothing, circular motion. Grant had re-entered the now crowded office with his brother, John.

"Somebody, say something!" Karmyn shouted. The silence in the room was driving her crazy.

"Sister, it's okay to express whatever feelings you are having. We want to give you time to process everything," Poe said.

"Process what? My ex-husband, a man I never really knew, tried to extort money from me by playing on my emotions. Am I that naïve that he thought I would fall for it?" Karmyn asked to no one in particular.

"Sister, no one believes that." Kyna looked around the room for support.

"Karmyn, your sister is right. Vincent was a master manipulator, and his co-conspirators were pushing him on. The man has a gambling and alcohol problem. None of that has anything to do with you," John spoke. John Hawkins was the youngest brother of the Hawkins siblings and considered family. John and Carlton had arrived just before the police. They provided the missing information to the entire plot.

"Yeah, well, right now, I feel like an idiot. I knew to keep my guard up. Even today, I kicked Vincent out of my office. But he almost had me with that phone call. I almost fell into the trap, and that is why I am so angry at myself."

Karmyn allowed her siblings and their significant others to

comfort her. Someone had ordered dinner from the corner deli, and her family was trying to keep her spirits lifted. After a while, everyone began departing, leaving Karmyn and Nick alone.

*****

"Are you ready to head home?" Nick asked.

"Not yet," she answered, looking off into the distance.

Nick was first elated that she hadn't kicked him out, and second, he felt proud of how she handled herself with the police. What he didn't like was how she was behaving now. Karmyn was quiet and still processing the events that took place. She was placing blame on herself for the outcome of the actions of a few greedy people.

He moved to sit beside Karmyn and saw her briefly flinch. Nick needed to know what was going on in her mind.

"Talk to me, please. What are you thinking?" Nick asked in a soft voice.

She continued staring straight ahead. Nick didn't want to push the issue, but she needed to talk. He waited a few minutes, then asked again.

"I can't help but feel like I bear some responsibility about today's events," she sighed.

"How is that?"

"He was my husband. He needed help, and I left. I divorced him. If only I had tried harder in my marriage, maybe convinced him to seek counseling."

Nick was shocked that this was where her mind was going. How could he convince her that Vincent's issues were his alone? Maybe she could have gotten him to seek help, but how long would she have stayed in the marriage with unrequited love.

"Karmyn, you were just surrounded by a room full of people

who love you. No one believes that there was anything you could have done to prevent what happened here." Nick gently reached for her hand, and she pulled back slightly before allowing him to touch her. Once he held her hand, she squeezed tightly and then let her tears fall.

Nick didn't know what to do except to hold her until she was ready to talk. She cried in his arms for over thirty minutes. She finally looked up and into Nick's eyes. He saw so much guilt and sorrow there. They stayed this way, gazing at each other for several minutes.

"Nick, we need to talk about us."

Oh no, the "we need to talk" speech. Nick didn't know whether to be concerned or pleased that she was ready to talk. His eyes never left hers, and he squeezed her hand to give her the confidence to continue.

"I'm no good at this relationship thing. Mostly because my only experience just tried to play me for money. I feel completely exposed and unsure of myself. Especially now when it comes to you. We have had some good times over the past few months, and I don't want that to end. But that is all I want right now, a friend. I can't handle a relationship."

Nick nodded his support, unable to say anything. This is what she wanted. More importantly, this is what she needed. His mother told him once that a good relationship started with a solid foundation. It wasn't too long ago that this woman hated him. If he honestly wanted a relationship with her, he needed to focus on the foundation, and that was their friendship.

"Karmyn, I won't lie to you. I am really feeling you. But your friendship means more to me than anything. Whatever you need from me, I will do it within my power."

She smiled for the first time since the ordeal began. Nick hoped that she would eventually come around and accept his role in her life as more than a friend. That hope was for the future.

Chapter 14

Karleigh and Simon's annual family backyard barbecue was in full swing. Everyone was there, including the barbers from The Sharper Image and the stylists from Serenity. Mr. and Mrs. Hawkins had arrived from New York and were engaged in a spirited card game with Mr. and Mrs. Sharp.

Echo and Whisper openly had their eyes on Nigel and Nathan. Kyra Hammond was helping her daughters prepare the food tables while Mr. Hammond and Simon were manning the grill. There were games of cornhole happening at the back of the yard, and someone issued a challenge of horseshoes.

This is what family fun was supposed to look like. Simon carried over the last of the chicken from the grill and began gathering people around.

"Who is missing?" Poe asked.

"We are waiting on Nick and Karmyn," Simon answered.

Karmyn was in therapy and happily enjoying being friends with Nick. The family still considered them dating, but they were taking things one day at a time.

"Don't start without us," Karmyn yelled as she entered the backyard through the side fence.

"Where is Nick?" Simon asked.

"Right here, sorry we are late. We stopped to pick up a few bottles of champagne."

"Champagne? What are we celebrating?" Poe asked.

"I've no idea. Karmyn made me do it. And I had to get the good stuff. Somebody is reimbursing me for this." Nick laughed.

"Now that everyone is here let us bow our heads for grace," Mr. Hammond announced.

Mr. Hammond gave grace, and everyone started digging into the food. Once everyone had their plates filled to the top with food, Simon decided it was the best time to make announcements.

"This is just the first of many family fun day barbecues that my wife and I plan to host. We love when our family and extended family can get together and just love on each other." Simon was getting a little emotional when he asked that everyone fill their glasses with champagne.

"Karleigh, please join me. We have something that we want to announce." He beamed down into his wife's face. "We are having a baby!"

Screams came from all over the yard.

"Wait a minute, wait just one minute." Kyna stood on a chair, supported by her husband. "This champagne is not for you, dear sister. It was for us." She looked lovingly into Morgan's eyes before continuing. "Because we are pregnant too!"

Kyra couldn't stop crying. Eventually, her husband had to take her inside the house to calm down. Mrs. Hawkins held on to her oldest son and Kyna for an undetermined amount of time. She then looked around for her two youngest children, but they had disappeared.

Nick walked over to his brothers and laughed. "See how happy you two could be."

"Nathan, is he talking to us? Because I could have sworn his woman was over there." Nigel laughed and walked far away from his parents before they got any ideas.

"You know, big brother," Nathan started. "I'm not afraid of love. I'm just not sure the woman I am supposed to spend my life with is in this city or this state. What if she is in Brazil and I haven't been there to find her yet. I'm just keeping my eyes open to all possibilities.

Nick knew, understanding his brother's logic may cause a slight brain bleed, so he left it alone. They would figure it out soon enough. He walked back toward the sisters, who had finally stopped their crying. Happiness was supposed to feel like this, and this was all that Nick ever wanted.

Scriptures of Hope

Ephesians 1:18 I pray that the eyes of your heart may be enlightened in order that you may know the hope to which he has called you, the riches of his glorious inheritance in his holy people,

Isaiah 40:31 but those who hope in the LORD will renew their strength. They will soar on wings like eagles; they will run and not grow weary, they will walk and not be faint.

Jeremiah 29:11 For I know the plans I have for you," declares the LORD, "plans to prosper you and not to harm you, plans to give you hope and a future.

Psalm 71:14 As for me, I will always have hope; I will praise you more and more.

Psalm 130:5 I wait for the LORD, my whole being waits, and in his word I put my hope.

Romans 5:5 And hope does not put us to shame, because God's love has been poured out into our hearts through the Holy Spirit, who has been given to us.

Romans 8:24 For in this hope we were saved. But hope that is seen is no hope at all. Who hopes for what they already have?

Romans 15:13 May the God of hope fill you with all joy and peace as you trust in him, so that you may overflow with hope by the power of the Holy Spirit.

ABOUT THE AUTHOR

Award-winning Christian Fiction/Romance author Lisa Washington is a Detroit native and currently residing in Georgia with her family. Washington earned her bachelor's degree in public relations from Wayne State University in Detroit, MI and a master's degree in business administration from Averett University in Danville, VA. It wasn't until she suffered from the stresses of a Ph.D, program that she decided, if she had to write 75-page papers, they would be something she truly enjoyed writing.

Two years later, Washington was accepted into the Master of Fine Arts program for creative writing at Butler University in Indianapolis, IN. She applied with a terrible first draft of her first published novel, "When You Least Expect It." Washington completed her program in 2016.

Washington went on to win the 2018 African American Literary Award Show, Best Christian Fiction Award for *When You Least Expect It* and the 2020 Author Elite Award, Clean Romance for *Love Lifted Me.*

Washington also served several years in the US Navy before attending college. Washington credits having a strong faith in God and trusting He had a plan for her life. Her faith is also what drives her to write Christian fiction and romance. She is often quoted saying, "If it were not for God, I don't know where I would be today."

Lisa Washington and her husband are the co-founders of The Washington Way LLC, including Washington Way Financial, Washington Way Publishing, Washington Way Travel, and Ms. Lisa Weddings.

ALSO BY LISA WASHINGTON

THE FAITH SERIES

When You Least Expect It

More Than You Know

Love Lifted Me

MY SISTERS KEEPER SERIES

Karleigh – A Story of Faith

Kaleigh – A Story of Patience

Kyna – A Story of Love

Karmyn – A Story of Hope

I hope you enjoyed reading about Karmyn and Nick. Having Hope doesn't mean losing Faith. Forgiveness is also a part of having that Hope for the future.

Stay connected with us for new releases, exclusive offers, free online reads and so much more.

Subscribe to my newsletter
www.authorlisawashington.com

Don't forget to follow and like us on
Facebook - @authorlisawashington
IG - @authorlisawashington
Pinterest - authorlisawashington

9 781953 205049